The Smell of Fear

Pete crouched on Alex's window ledge with his nose to the screen, glad that Alex liked fresh air at night even in winter. Pete inhaled deeply as he peered through the dark trees toward the house next door. His fur rose along the ridge of his back. He smelled fear, sharp animal fear, although he couldn't tell what kind of animal was in danger.

Something was wrong at Mary's house.

A van stood in the neighbor's driveway, its rear door open.

As Pete watched, a figure hurried to the van and placed a large object inside. Pete tried to slide the window open farther, but it held fast. Frustrated, he pawed at the window.

The figure returned to the house and came back a few seconds later carrying another object. It's the burglar, Pete realized. He's stealing things out of Mary's house!

SPY
CAT

OTHER BOOKS BY PEG KEHRET

Abduction!

Cages

Danger at the Fair

Don't Tell Anyone

Earthquake Terror

The Ghost's Grave

Horror at the Haunted Museum

I'm Not Who You Think I Am

Night of Fear

Nightmare Mountain

Searching for Candlestick Park

Sisters Long Ago

The Stranger Next Door

Terror at the Zoo

PEG KEHRET
AND PETE THE CAT

SPY
CAT

SLEUTH
PUFFIN

PUFFIN BOOKS
Published by the Penguin Group
Penguin Young Readers Group, 345 Hudson Street, New York, New York 10014, U.S.A.
Penguin Group (Canada), 90 Eglinton Avenue East, Suite 700,
Toronto, Ontario, Canada M4P 2Y3 (a division of Pearson Penguin Canada Inc.)
Penguin Books Ltd, 80 Strand, London WC2R 0RL, England
Penguin Ireland, 25 St Stephen's Green, Dublin 2, Ireland
(a division of Penguin Books Ltd)
Penguin Group (Australia), 250 Camberwell Road, Camberwell, Victoria 3124, Australia
(a division of Pearson Australia Group Pty Ltd)
Penguin Books India Pvt Ltd, 11 Community Centre,
Panchsheel Park, New Delhi - 110 017, India
Penguin Group (NZ), 67 Apollo Drive, Rosedale, North Shore 0632, New Zealand
(a division of Pearson New Zealand Ltd)
Penguin Books (South Africa) (Pty) Ltd, 24 Sturdee Avenue,
Rosebank, Johannesburg 2196, South Africa

Registered Offices: Penguin Books Ltd, 80 Strand, London WC2R 0RL, England

First published in the United States of America by Dutton Children's Books,
a division of Penguin Young Readers Group, 2003
Published by Puffin Books, a division of Penguin Young Readers Group, 2004
This Sleuth edition published by Puffin Books, a division of Penguin Young Readers Group, 200

9 10 8

Copyright © Peg Kehret, 2003
All rights reserved

CIP Data is available
Puffin Books ISBN 978-0-14-241219-0

Printed in the United States of America

True friends enrich our lives and encourage the best in us.

To Larry Karp, a fine writer, who lets me play with his musical animals

To Myra Karp, whose many talents include seven-layer chocolate cakes and the world's best pizza

To Erin Karp, cat-loving attorney and honorary daughter
—P.K.

To my friends, Daisy and Molly
—PETE

SPY
CAT

Prologue

*E*very animal, human or other, needs work that matters. I am Pete the cat, and I have more than one important responsibility. I'm an excellent lap-warmer, a fearless protector of my family, and a published author. You are reading my second book, and I must say that this part of my job doesn't get any easier.

When I first approached the keyboard, I had no desire for literary fame. I wanted to write because I had heard that every computer has a mouse. Then I got interested in the story that my person, Peg, was working on, so I began to add my ideas to hers. We ended up writing a novel together and we had fun doing it.

When I first discovered that my big white-and-brown cat, Pete, knows how to read and write, I was shocked. His papers from the humane society said "good with children," but there was no hint of any literary ability, so you can imagine my surprise when he began adding pages to the book I was writing.

I know how to talk, too, but she hasn't yet learned to understand me. Humans think they are smarter than the rest of us animals when any cat knows it's the other way around.

In the first book that Pete and I coauthored, *The Stranger Next Door*, I wrote the parts about people and he wrote the parts about the cat. We did that with this book, too. His parts are in italics so you can tell which ones they are.

Actually, the cat's parts are in italics because they are the most important.

I thought Pete would get tired of writing after the first book, but when I started this story I left my computer on at night, in case he wanted to add something. Sure enough, the next morning there were two pages told from the cat's point of view.

She hasn't grown tired of writing, so why would I? Writing is challenging, fun, and satisfying—like catching a fly. I used to spend my nights batting at catnip-scented balls and trying to wake up my people. Now I write novels because novelists get to go to bookstores and put their paw prints in their books. No one ever got famous by playing with catnip balls.

All of the characters in this book except one are fictional. I'm sure you'll be able to tell which one is real.

These was no need to make up a cat character when a clever, courageous, and capable cat like me was willing to be in the story. If you ever need to describe me, remember the three C's.

It should really be four C's—add one for "corpulent."

Corpulent! There isn't an ounce of fat on me. That uninformed veterinarian who suggested diet cat food doesn't know muscle when he sees it.

Having a cat as my coauthor has worked well. The only problem we had on this book was when Pete kept changing the cover so that his name was in bigger letters than my name. Our editor vetoed that.

I did most of the work, so I should get most of the credit, but I settled for extra kitty num-num.

Enough of this explanation. Here is the second story that Pete and I wrote together.

1

Alex Kendrill was pouring cat food into Pete's bowl when his little brother, Benjie, raced into the house.

"The new neighbors are here," Benjie shouted, "and we're going to like them!" The door slammed shut behind him.

Pete, Alex's big white-and-brown cat, quit rubbing against Alex's legs and ran under the table. He peered out, hoping Benjie would leave so Pete could eat breakfast in peace. Pete liked Benjie, but he didn't like all the loud noises that Benjie made.

"Do they have boys?" Alex asked.

Alex's family had been one of the first to move into a new housing development. Every time another family moved in, Benjie hoped they would have boys his age, but it hadn't happened yet.

Benjie took two cookies out of the cookie jar and a

small can of apple juice from the refrigerator. "So far I only saw a girl and an old woman," he said as he popped open the juice. "Maybe the boys are coming with their dad."

"How do you know we're going to like them?"

"Because they have a whole bunch of animals."

"What kind of animals?" Alex asked.

Pete's tail swished back and forth. He hoped a pack of dogs didn't move in next door. Even though Pete was kept inside, he escaped whenever he could. If dogs lived next door, he'd have to be more cautious.

"I didn't actually see any animals," Benjie admitted, "but I saw a cage with a blanket over it, and some carriers like the one we use when we take Pete to the vet."

Pete growled. He wished Benjie wouldn't talk about the vet.

Benjie grabbed his binoculars and the backpack that he called his spy kit. "I'll be out in front," he said.

"Mom and Dad don't want you spying on the neighbors," Alex said.

"How else will we know if they have boys or not?"

Benjie went out, letting the door bang behind him.

Pete returned to his breakfast.

Alex turned on the computer. While he waited to get connected to the Internet, he read his homework assignment: "Write three paragraphs or more about the history of Oklahoma."

With any luck he would find everything he needed to know on the Internet. He could finish the assignment quickly and spend the morning on more important things, such as asking Rocky to come over to shoot baskets.

When his search results appeared on the screen, he clicked on the most promising site and began to read. Oklahoma history turned out to be more interesting than he had expected. He especially liked a picture that showed an oil well on the grounds of the state capitol building.

Half an hour later Alex was printing out his report when he heard four knocks at the back door in the special rhythm that Rocky always used. "Come on in!" Alex yelled.

"Alex?"

"I'm in the family room." Alex shut off the printer and put his assignment in a folder. "What's up?" he said as he heard Rocky enter the room.

"Someone broke into our house! We were burglarized!"

Alex turned to his friend. "When? What happened?"

"Today. This morning." Rocky looked pale, the way he had when he'd caught the flu. "Mother and Blake and I went out for breakfast, and when we got home our back door had been kicked in. Whoever did it took both our television sets and our computer and Blake's new camera and some cash." His voice trembled, as if he couldn't quite catch his breath.

"Did you call the police?" Alex asked.

"The sheriff just left. He wrote down everything we're missing and said to call if we discover anything else that was taken."

"Do you have any idea who did it?"

"No, but whoever it was must have seen us leave because we were only gone a little over an hour. We ate breakfast at Mad Dog's Diner, then picked up some paint at the hardware store. When we got home, the back door was open."

Alex's stomach felt queasy. Three months ago an arsonist had set fires in the neighborhood and had nearly killed Alex. The arsonist got caught, but it had been the most horrible experience of Alex's life. He had barely begun to feel safe again, and now this happened.

Pete went to Rocky and rubbed against his ankles. Rocky had saved Pete's life during the fire, and Pete would never forget it.

"The sheriff went across the street to talk to the family who moved in last week," Rocky said, "to see if anyone saw a car or people at our house while we were gone. I need to get back. I wanted to tell you what happened, but when I tried to call, your line was busy for a long time."

"I was on the Internet, doing my homework."

"Do you want to come over to my house?"

"I'm watching Benjie while Mom and Dad buy groceries; I can't leave unless I take him along." Alex didn't have to explain why that wouldn't be a good idea. Rocky knew all about Benjie's spy games. "Right now he's busy spying on the new people who are moving in next door. You can stay here, if you want to."

"Maybe I'll come over later," Rocky said. "I want to go home and find out if the sheriff got any leads. I'm kind of shook up over this."

"I don't blame you. Let me know what happens."

Rocky started to leave, then turned to look back. "Keep your doors locked," he said.

"I will."

Pete jumped to the window ledge and watched Rocky ride his bike down the driveway. That burglar had better not try to break in here. If he does, he'll get more than he bargained for, Pete thought.

I'll bite him in the ankle. I'll climb his leg and shred his pants. He'll have more holes in his backside than a piece of Swiss cheese.

Alex stared at the door for a few seconds after Rocky left. Had someone been watching Rocky's house, waiting for his family to leave? Would the burglars return to Valley View Estates?

He walked to the front door and checked to be sure it was locked. Then he paced around the house, angry at whoever had broken into Rocky's home. It made him furious to see his friend so upset, and he felt helpless to do

11

anything about it. Why did there have to be such bad people in the world?

He was still fuming when Benjie came in the kitchen door, followed by a girl who appeared to be about the same age as Alex.

"This is Mary," Benjie said. "She's our new neighbor and she wants to use our telephone."

Alex introduced himself, then showed Mary the phone.

"Do you have a directory that I could use?" she asked. "I need to call the electric company. Our power isn't on yet; it was supposed to get turned on yesterday. The phone company is coming this afternoon, but Gramma's afraid if we wait until then to call, it'll be too late to get power today."

Alex opened the cupboard where the phone book was kept and handed the directory to Mary. He wanted to tell Benjie about the burglary, but he didn't trust his brother not to take his spy kit and head straight for Rocky's house.

Pete jumped to the floor and walked toward the girl. Even though noisy Benjie was still in the room, Pete was curious about this visitor. She looked and smelled like someone who loved animals.

"What a beautiful cat," Mary said.

Pete went closer.

"This is Pete," Alex said.

Mary smiled at Pete. "He's a big one," she said.

While Mary looked up the number Pete sniffed at the hem of her jeans. He rubbed his face on one of her shoes.

When she finished her call, Mary let Pete sniff her hand.

Pete smelled soap and bread and some kind of animal— not a cat or a dog, something different. He inhaled deeply, trying to recognize the scent.

"He probably smells Pearly, the possum. I put fresh water in her cage before I came over."

"I never heard of a possum for a pet," Alex said. "The only possum I ever saw was dead on the side of the road."

Pete growled. He wished humans wouldn't talk about such horrible things.

"She isn't a pet," Mary said. "The car ahead of us hit her, and the driver didn't bother to stop. Gramma and I could see she was still alive, so we took her to a wildlife rehabilitation center. Gramma's a licensed foster parent for the center and for another animal rescue group. The center's vets were able to save Pearly, but one front paw hasn't healed yet. As soon as it does, she'll be released back into the wild."

Pete rubbed against Mary's ankles, purring loudly. Anyone who would rescue an injured animal was Pete's friend.

"I wanted to keep Pearly and call her Pearly the permanent possum," Mary said, "but Gramma says it's unkind to keep a wild animal in a cage. Pearly will be happier in her natural habitat."

13

"I thought for sure you had pets," Benjie said.

"There are usually two or three other critters living with us until they can be released in the wild or put up for adoption. Right now we have a cat named Howley Girl, who has a cold and has to be isolated, and a dog named Rufus, who had one leg amputated. He'll be with us until his stump heals."

"Gross," said Benjie.

"Rufus isn't gross," Mary said, "but the boys who used him for target practice are." She gave the telephone directory back to Alex. "Thanks for letting me use your phone."

"Do you need help carrying stuff into the house?" Alex asked. "I'm not doing anything this morning except watching Benjie while my parents are at the grocery store."

"I don't need watching," Benjie said. "I'll help, too."

"That would be great," Mary said. "A moving company is bringing the furniture, but we packed everything else in boxes ourselves, and it all has to get unloaded. Gramma is too independent to admit it, but I can tell she's getting tired."

Alex wrote a quick note for his parents. "Mom and Dad: Benjie and I are next door helping the new neighbors move in." He hesitated, tempted to add the news about the burglary, but he decided to wait and tell it in person.

Benjie set his binoculars and his spy backpack on the kitchen table then followed Alex and Mary out the door.

Alex reached back, caught the door before it slammed, and turned the lock button. If he needed to get into the house before Mom and Dad returned, he could use the spare key that was hidden in the garage.

Yesterday he would have left the door open and not thought anything about it, but not today. Not after what had happened only two streets away.

It's Saturday, Alex thought, and my homework's done, and the new neighbors are interesting people. I shouldn't have a care in the world, but instead I'm tense and anxious.

Burglars take more than household goods. They also steal peace of mind.

2

As they walked toward the rental truck, Mary said, "I'll start school on Monday at Hilltop School."

"That's where we go," Benjie said. "I'm in first grade."

"What grade are you in?" Alex asked Mary.

"Sixth."

"So am I."

"Do you like it?" Mary asked.

Alex shrugged. "School is school. It's okay, I guess, except for all the homework."

"I love school," Mary said. "Especially science."

"I love school, too," Benjie said. "Especially recess."

As they approached Mary's house, a handsome golden retriever hobbled toward them on three legs, wagging his tail.

"This is Rufus," Mary said.

The dog licked Alex's hand and submitted to a hug from Benjie.

"Amazing, isn't it?" Mary said. "He still trusts and loves people after all he's been through."

Mary introduced her grandmother, Mrs. Sunburg. Then they all set to work carrying cardboard boxes from the truck to the house.

The three kids chatted as they worked.

"Gramma tried to save money on our move," Mary said, "so she hired two men who call themselves Muscle Men Movers. They weren't too careful when they loaded our things. One of them dropped my desk, and we're lucky it wasn't ruined. I don't think they have much experience."

"How did she know about them?" Alex asked.

"From an ad stuck on the bulletin board outside the post office. I think we should have used an established moving company. They were supposed to follow us here, but we've been here over an hour, and they haven't arrived yet."

"Maybe they got lost."

Mary sighed. "Gramma is too trusting," she said. "She's always trying to help out somebody in need. She hired those jokers because she thought they needed the money, not because they were qualified. I hope we see our furniture again."

Mrs. Sunburg came out in time to hear that last comment. "You must have faith in your fellowman," she said. "Think good of others, and they'll live up to your opinion of them."

"I hope you're right," Mary said, "but I don't have too high an opinion of anyone who calls Pearly a stupid rat. That guy even said we had to drive Pearly over here ourselves because he 'didn't want a stupid rat's cage' in his truck. As if I would have entrusted Pearly to those two."

"We had a rat in my classroom last year," Benjie said. "His name was Randolph and we took turns cleaning his cage. He wasn't stupid, though. He was smart. He learned his name and he learned to run back in his cage whenever the bell rang."

"Pearly probably isn't as smart as a rat," Mary said. "Possums have small brains. But that's no reason to dislike her. Did you know that possums are marsupials? They carry their young in pouches, the way kangaroos do."

Every few minutes, a loud cat howl came from behind a closed door on the second floor and echoed through the house.

"I can hear Howley Girl," Alex said. "You gave her the right name."

"She's shut in the upstairs bathroom until we finish moving in," Mary said. "We were afraid she'd slip outside and get lost."

"Can I go in and see her?" Benjie asked.

"You'd better not, since you have a cat at home. Cat colds are contagious, and I wouldn't want Pete to get sick."

It was noon when they hauled the last box inside. Muscle Men Movers still hadn't arrived with the furniture.

By then Alex knew that Mary's parents both worked for a nonprofit organization that provided medical supplies to needy people in other countries.

"They get home twice a year to visit," Mary said. "I live with Gramma and her critters."

Alex didn't think he'd like that arrangement. Even though Mom nagged him to clean his room and eat more vegetables, and Dad had strict rules about no TV until Alex's homework was done, Alex knew he would miss his parents terribly if they were gone for months at a time.

"You must have lunch with us," Mrs. Sunburg said as she took the top off a large cooler. "I brought more food than Mary and I can eat." She made each of them a sandwich while Mary poured orange juice into glasses.

"Saturday is my main spy day," Benjie said as they ate. "Today I'm going to look for flying green panthers. Their tails spin around like helicopter propellers, and the panthers rise up and hover over the treetops."

Mrs. Sunburg looked startled.

Mary laughed.

"The panthers are hard to spot," Benjie went on, "because they're the same color as the leaves, and their tails don't make any noise. I'll need to use my binoculars."

"Let me know if you see one," Mary said. "I'd like to see it, too."

"I will," Benjie promised. "Maybe I'll even show you my secret spy hideout."

"That's an honor," Alex told Mary.

Mrs. Sunburg said, "I shouldn't think there would be much work for a spy in Valley View Estates. We chose this house because it's so peaceful here. What a relief to be out in the country, away from all the big-city crime."

"We've had trouble here, too," Alex said.

"I know about the arson fires," Mrs. Sunburg said. "We got this house at a bargain price because it had to be rebuilt."

"Is there any dessert?" Benjie asked.

"Benjie!" Alex said. "That isn't polite."

"I'm afraid not," Mrs. Sunburg said. "I'm trying to lose weight, and Mary doesn't have a sweet tooth."

"We need to get home, anyway," Alex said. "Thanks for lunch."

Benjie ran on ahead. Alex knew he was heading for the cookie jar.

Alex lingered long enough to tell Mrs. Sunburg and Mary about the burglary at Rocky's house. He didn't like to worry them, but he wanted them to be cautious.

When Alex got home, his parents were watching a television news broadcast while they ate sandwiches. Benjie sat at the table with an open package of frosted animal cookies in front of him.

Ordinarily Alex would have ignored the news and gone for the cookies, but as he walked in he heard the announcer say, "Last night a burglary in Hilltop almost turned deadly."

Alex looked at the TV screen. Valley View Estates was at the edge of Hilltop! Was the announcer going to tell about the burglary at Rocky's house? But that had been this morning, not last night. There must have been another burglary in the area.

When the commercials finally ended, the announcer said, "A cat burglar struck the small rural community of Hilltop last night. Darren Ludwig, who lives alone in a rented house, awakened around two A.M. and heard someone in his kitchen. When he went to investigate, he was struck on the head and knocked unconscious. By the time Mr. Ludwig came to and called for help, the burglar had removed many valuables from the home. Mr. Ludwig has a concussion but is expected to make a full recovery."

Alex felt a chill down the back of his neck. He wondered if the person who had hit the man on the head last night had also been in Rocky's house this morning.

"There has been a rash of burglaries in rural areas in recent weeks," the announcer said. "The cat burglar, who entered the Hilltop home by breaking a window, usually comes at night, although there have been some daytime burglaries, too. Police don't know if the same person is responsible for all the thefts. Everyone is reminded to keep their doors and windows locked."

"Why is there never any good news?" Mr. Kendrill said. "Every day we hear about murders and wars and now another burglary."

"Why do cats always get the blame?" Pete said. "Nobody ever talks about dog burglars."

"Burglars broke into Rocky's house," Alex said.

"They did?" Mr. Kendrill said. "When?"

"This morning."

"Was anyone hurt?" Mrs. Kendrill asked. "Were Rocky and his parents at home?"

Alex told his shocked family what had happened. When he finished, he heard a sniffling sound and saw a tear roll down Benjie's cheek.

"What if the burglars come here?" Benjie said.

"They'll regret it," Pete said. He went to his scratching post and began sharpening his claws.

"Oh, honey, they won't come here," Mrs. Kendrill said.

"How do you know?" Benjie said. "They went to Rocky's house. They might come to our house and try to steal Pete."

"Let them try," said Pete.

Mrs. Kendrill went to Benjie and hugged him.

"The burglars might come to my school," Benjie said.

Mr. Kendrill pointed the remote control at the TV and switched to a channel that played cartoons.

"If burglars come to Hilltop School," Alex said, "the whole sixth grade will catch them and tie them up." He flexed his muscles and made a tough-guy face.

Benjie started watching the cartoon, but Alex caught

22

the worried glance that his parents exchanged and knew these burglaries were making them anxious, too.

"If the burglar comes here," Pete said, "I'll chase him away. I'll sneak up behind him and bite him in the rear. He won't be able to sit down for a week."

"Alex," Mr. Kendrill said, "did you remember to feed Pete this morning?"

"Yes. I think he's meowing because he wants to go out."

"I'm not meowing," Pete said. "I'm speaking perfect English."

"Want a cookie?" Benjie offered the package to Alex.

Alex shook his head. "No, thanks."

He wasn't hungry anymore.

He got Pete's harness and leash. It was time for what Alex called "cat meditation hour." Maybe if he stood around outside while Pete ate grass and watched the birds, he would feel less jittery.

The purpose of Pete's outings was to give him exercise, but Pete, after begging to go out, often sat in one spot the whole time he was outside. Usually, when Alex stood quietly in the grass beside Pete, he felt calm. The rustling of the wind in the trees, the movements of the birds, and the sun on his shoulders were soothing and made any problems seem less urgent.

Not today. Today the world seemed less safe than it had been yesterday. Even the trees seemed to whisper ominous warnings, and the sudden flights of the birds hinted at danger. Instead of closing his eyes and letting the sun warm his face as he usually did, Alex found himself looking over his shoulder.

Benjie is right, he thought. The burglars could come to our house next.

3

When the cartoons ended, Benjie put two cookies in his jacket pocket and hung his binoculars around his neck. He walked to his secret hideout, which was a clump of huckleberry bushes on a vacant corner lot. He dropped to his hands and knees, then backed into the bushes until only his face stuck out.

He pressed his binoculars to his eyes and turned his head slowly from side to side. He had a good view of Valley View Drive, the main street into the housing development where he lived. He could see any vehicles that turned onto his street, Elm Lane, and any that went past Elm, toward Rocky's street.

He had planned to watch for flying green panthers today, but that was before he found out that Rocky's house had been burglarized. Now Benjie was watching for burglars or kidnappers or other bad guys.

Benjie knew Mom and Dad were upset about the burglaries. They had warned him twice not to talk to strangers, as if he didn't know that already, and had made him promise not to go beyond the corner.

Dad had even dug in the junk drawer for the whistle that he used when he coached Alex's basketball team and had insisted that Benjie wear the whistle around his neck when he was outdoors alone.

"You can blow it if you ever get lost," Dad had said.

Benjie knew Dad really meant, you can blow it if you ever need help. Those burglars were bad guys. If they were bad enough to kick in Rocky's door and steal things, and to hit that man on the head, maybe they'd do other bad stuff, like blow up houses or kidnap children. Benjie intended to stay watchful.

Every time a car drove down the street, Benjie looked at it through his binoculars. There wasn't a lot of traffic, since Valley View Estates was several miles from any city. Only the small town of Hilltop was farther up the road. After Hilltop, the paved road ended. A narrow dirt road continued for a time, then quit altogether.

Benjie saw an old dented truck turn down Elm Lane. It said MUSCLE MEN MOVERS on the side. Good, he thought. Mary's furniture is here. He saw two neighbors who lived on Alder Court, the next street over from the Kendrills'. They were both driving down Valley View, headed for the highway; half an hour later one of them returned.

Next he spotted a vehicle he did not recognize: a mud-splattered pickup truck that sat up higher over the tires than it was meant to. The truck turned onto Elm but made a U-turn right away. It stopped at the corner and sat there with the engine idling. Benjie fiddled with his binoculars, focusing on the truck.

The driver was a young man wearing a red baseball cap. The woman who sat in the passenger's side had long hair pulled back into a ponytail. Both of them looked around, peering over their shoulders as if they wanted to be sure they were alone.

Benjie glanced up and down the street. He saw nobody. As he looked at the truck again, the woman opened her door and leaned out. Benjie wondered if she was carsick. As he trained the binoculars on her, she sat up again and slammed the door shut.

Instantly, the tires squealed. The driver took off as if he were in a race, leaving a black puff of exhaust fumes behind him.

As the truck turned the corner and sped away, Benjie looked back at where the truck had stopped.

A brown cardboard box about a foot square sat in the street, right beside where the truck had been.

The woman wasn't carsick, Benjie thought. She leaned out to put that box on the street, and then they drove away fast and left it behind.

Possibilities flew through Benjie's mind like a video on fast-forward. It's a bomb, Benjie thought. It's a bomb on a timer and it will explode. He looked at the box again. But why would anyone blow up an empty street? Benjie had seen enough news broadcasts to know that terrorists who set off bombs always chose crowded places where they could do as much damage as possible.

Benjie started to crawl out of his secret place. He would run home and tell Mom and Dad about the box. They could call the police and let them come and get the box.

He stopped as a new idea occurred to him. Maybe the box was filled with illegal drugs. The people in the truck are drug dealers and this is how they distribute the drugs. Probably another car would drive up soon and take the box away. If so, Benjie needed to stay in his spy place and watch so he could give the police a description of the car and the people who picked up the box.

He crawled back in the huckleberry bushes and waited. He opened his backpack and removed the notebook and pencil. Although Benjie knew how to read, he didn't write very well yet, so he couldn't write down a description of the truck; he would have to remember what it looked like.

He knew his numbers, though, and he knew the alphabet. If a car stopped near the box, Benjie would get the license number and print it in his notebook.

Even without the number he could give the police a good description of the truck. While he waited for another car to come he practiced what he would say.

He focused the binoculars on the box again.

The top of the box moved! Benjie leaned forward.

The box moved again. One of the top flaps, which was tucked inside the other flap, kept going up and down as if something alive was inside the box trying to get out.

Benjie crept out of the bushes. He looked in all directions and saw no vehicles. He ran to the box and crouched beside it.

"Mrow."

The sound was so soft that it took a second for Benjie to realize what he had heard.

"Mrow." A tiny paw poked up in the space where the edges of the flaps were folded together.

Benjie opened the box and looked inside.

A small black-and-tan-striped kitten clambered up the side of the box and toppled into the street. Benjie scooped the kitten up and held it close. "It's okay, kitty," he whispered. "You're safe now."

Outrage flooded through Benjie. Those people had deliberately shut the kitten in a box and left the box in the street. What if a car had come along and run over the box? What if Benjie hadn't seen the box? A big dog might have smelled it and gotten the box open and killed the kitten. If no one had seen the box, the kitten could have starved to death!

He held the kitten close and ran for home, carrying the empty box in his other hand.

As soon as Alex finished Pete's outing, he called Rocky. "Did the sheriff learn anything?" he asked. "Did the new neighbors see who was at your house?"

"No. The new people weren't home when it happened. The sheriff thinks the burglar drove up our driveway, loaded our stuff out, and was gone in less than ten minutes."

In his mind, Alex saw Rocky's driveway, which curved around to the back side of the house. A car or truck parked at the end next to the kitchen door wouldn't be visible from the street.

All of the houses in Valley View Estates were on large lots, most of them wooded. People here liked their privacy, but the secluded homes made things easier for burglars.

"We heard on the news that another house in Hilltop got burglarized in the night and the thief knocked out the man who lived there."

"I know," Rocky said. "The sheriff told us about it."

"Do you want to sleep over at my house tonight?" Alex asked. "Mom and Dad said you can come anytime and eat dinner with us."

"Hold on a minute. I'll ask." A few seconds later, Rocky

said, "I'll be there in a little while, but I have to come home early in the morning. We're going skiing in the mountains tomorrow."

"Bring your sleeping bag; it's my turn to have the bed."

Rocky and Alex often spent the night together, and since both boys had only a single bed, they took turns sleeping on the floor.

Half an hour later, they were shooting baskets in Alex's driveway when Benjie dashed toward the house.

"I found a kitten," he yelled. "A truck came and I spied on it and the people put a box in the street and left it there and the box was moving and when I looked inside, there was a kitten!"

"A purple-and-gold kitten," Alex told Rocky as he dribbled toward the basket.

"One that plays the clarinet," Rocky said.

"While it flies over the trees." Alex shot, missed, and got his own rebound.

"Hey!" Rocky said, pointing to Benjie. "He really does have a kitten."

Alex dropped the basketball and looked at his brother. He and Rocky followed Benjie inside, where Benjie was telling his parents what had happened.

"Can I keep it?" Benjie said.

"We already have a cat," Mrs. Kendrill said.

"That's right," said Pete. "You already have the perfect

31

cat, who deserves to be the only pampered pet in the family, so don't even think about keeping that one."

"Pete is really Alex's cat," Benjie said. "Alex got to choose him at the humane society, and Alex got to name him, and Pete always sleeps with Alex. I want a pet of my own that I get to name."

"Pete is your cat, too," Mr. Kendrill said. "He's a family pet."

"Pete runs away or hides under the table when he sees me," Benjie said.

"Pete only hides when you shout or slam the door," Mrs. Kendrill said.

Which is most of the time, Pete thought.

"Please?" Benjie begged. "The kitten is so cute."

"All baby animals are cute," Mr. Kendrill said, "but they grow up quickly."

"I'm plenty of cat for two boys," Pete said. "Look at me!" He flopped on his side, then stretched out to his full length. "I could easily be two cats in one skin."

"Alex, did you take Pete for his walk?" Mrs. Kendrill asked.

"Yes. I had him outside for nearly an hour."

"Then why is he meowing?"

"Maybe he wants to see the kitten," Benjie said. He walked to where Pete lay and set the kitten on the floor.

Pete jumped to his feet.

"Oh, it is adorable," Mrs. Kendrill said. "Look at those tiny paws and that sweet face."

Pete looked. Then he sniffed. Pe-uw! The kitten was seriously in need of a good bath. Pete sighed. Knowing how inept the humans were in such matters, he supposed he would have to do it himself. He put one paw on the kitten's back, to hold it still, and began licking its ears.

4

L ook," Alex said. "Pete's grooming the kitten."

"He likes the kitty," Benjie said. "He wants us to keep it."

"I didn't say that," Pete said. "I'm only washing her so she won't stink." He continued licking the kitten's ears. When they were clean, he licked the kitten's face and chest.

The kitten held still, with its eyes closed. It didn't purr, but it kneaded its tiny claws in and out, the way Pete always did when he was happy.

"I wonder if it's a boy or a girl," Rocky said.

"It's a girl," Pete said.

Mrs. Kendrill picked up the kitten and looked under the tail. "It's a girl," she said.

"I told you that," Pete said. "Nobody listens to me."

Mrs. Kendrill didn't put the kitten down right away. Instead, she held it up under her chin and cuddled it.

"I'll take care of her," Benjie said. "I'll feed her and

brush her and she can sleep on my bed. I'll play with her every day."

"*She isn't getting any of MY food,*" Pete said.

"See?" Benjie said. "Pete wants to keep her, too."

That was just like a human, to twist words around so that they appeared to mean something entirely different from what the speaker had intended. Still, the kitten was small and helpless. Pete had been that little once, with no one to take care of him. If Alex hadn't selected him at the humane society, Pete didn't know where he would have ended up. Given Pete's own history, it didn't seem right to deny the kitten a home.

"*Oh, all right,*" Pete said. "*I suppose you can keep her if she stays out of my way—and out of my bowl.*"

"She's free," Benjie said. "We don't have to pay anything."

"Ha!" said Mr. Kendrill. "Fat chance."

"She's beautiful," Benjie said.

Alex looked at the kitten. She was two shades of brown, with black stripes. Alex had seen many cats who looked exactly like her. She was cute because she was so tiny, but Alex doubted she would ever be beautiful. He didn't say that, though.

"Kittens are a lot of trouble," Mr. Kendrill said. "Remember how Pete climbed the drapes when he was little? He walked on the piano keys at night and woke everyone up,

35

and he ran through the house all the time like a crazy thing, leaping on the furniture and knocking all the throw rugs out of place. Come to think of it, he still does that sometimes."

"Only when I have a cat fit," Pete said.

"For the most part, he grew out of all that wildness," Mrs. Kendrill said. "Pete's a wonderful cat now. He never climbs the drapes or walks on the piano keys anymore."

"I vote to keep the kitten," Benjie said.

"So do I," said Mrs. Kendrill.

"It's okay with me," said Alex.

"She can't eat any of my food," said Pete.

"I can see it doesn't matter how I vote," Mr. Kendrill said.

"I'm going to name her Elizabeth Van Lew," Benjie said.

"What?" said Mr. Kendrill.

"Elizabeth Van Lew was a spy during the Civil War. She took food and medicine to the prisoners, and they told her secrets about the Confederate Army, and then she told the Union Army what she knew. Elizabeth Van Lew was a hero."

Mrs. Kendrill looked dubious. "Elizabeth Van Lew," she said.

"That's quite a mouthful for such a small cat," Alex said. "I can't quite imagine calling her to come." He cupped his hands around his mouth and called, "Here, Elizabeth Van Lew. Here, Elizabeth Van Lew."

Benjie giggled. "That will be her real name," he said, "but I'll call her Lizzy."

"Could I hold her?" Rocky asked.

As Alex watched Rocky pet the kitten, he realized it was the first time today that his friend had smiled. Even when they had played "horse" with the basketball, Alex could tell that Rocky's heart wasn't in the game. The terrible knowledge that strangers had broken into his house and taken his family's personal property had hung over Rocky like a black cloud all day.

"If you had decided not to keep her," Rocky said, "I was going to ask if I could take her."

"You should have spoken up," Mr. Kendrill said.

"It's too late now," Benjie said.

Benjie no longer looked worried about the burglars, either. In fact, he was grinning as if it were his birthday.

Alex rubbed Pete behind the ears. "You're a good boy, Pete," he said, "to wash the kitten and not fight with her."

"She needs a role model, and who could do a better job of that than me?"

"He is a good boy," Mrs. Kendrill agreed. "Some cats refuse to accept another cat in their house. My friend Annette tried to take in a stray, and it was a disaster. For weeks, her cat did nothing but hiss and run away. Then the cats began fighting, and they both ended up at the vet with abscesses from scratching and biting each other. Talk about a catastrophe! Annette finally had to find a new home for the stray."

"The perfect word," Mr. Kendrill said. "Cat-astrophe."

"I liked disaster better," Pete said.

"Kitty num-num for you tonight," Alex told Pete.

"I'll need it," Pete said. *"Being a substitute parent will take a lot of energy."*

"Oh!" Mrs. Kendrill gasped. "I just thought of something!"

"What?" Mr. Kendrill asked.

"We need to take the kitten to the vet as soon as possible," Mrs. Kendrill said. "We don't know where she came from or whether she might have a disease that Pete could catch."

Alex picked up Pete and carried him away from the kitten.

"Kittens are usually immune to disease when they're this small," Mr. Kendrill said, "especially if the mother cat was vaccinated."

"She probably wasn't," Alex said, holding Pete closer. "People who care enough about their pets to get them vaccinated don't dump them on a street corner."

Mrs. Kendrill called the veterinary clinic, explained the situation, then said, "Thank you. We'll come right away."

After she hung up, she said, "They don't have any openings today, but they'll squeeze us in whenever we get there. Meanwhile, we're supposed to keep Lizzy away from Pete."

"I'll go outside," Pete offered.

Alex said, "I guess we should have thought of that before we let Pete wash her."

"If she isn't healthy," Mr. Kendrill warned, "we may not be able to keep her."

Benjie picked up Lizzy and held her tight, as if he were afraid someone was going to snatch the kitten away right then.

"She doesn't act sick," Pete said, *"and now that she's clean she smells all right."*

"The sooner the vet sees her, the better," Mrs. Kendrill said. "I'll take her now."

"Do you want Pete's carrier?" Alex asked.

"She can have it to keep," Pete said.

"Let's use the box she was in," Mrs. Kendrill said. "If she is sick, there's no sense getting germs on Pete's carrier."

"I want to hold her when we go," Benjie said. "She doesn't want to be shut in that dumb box again."

"She needs to be confined in the car, and when we go into the vet's office," Mrs. Kendrill said. "You know what it's like in that waiting room—dogs on leashes, and people talking, and phones ringing. Lizzy will be less frightened in her box."

"Then I'll put a towel in it so she's comfortable," Benjie said.

"Not one of the bathroom towels," Mrs. Kendrill said. "Take one from the rag pile."

Minutes later Mrs. Kendrill carried the box containing Lizzy to the car, with Benjie running ahead to open the door.

Alex and Rocky played a game of Clue while they waited for Mrs. Kendrill and Benjie to return. Rocky had just won when Mary knocked on the door.

"Did your power get turned on?" Alex asked, after he introduced Mary to his dad and Rocky.

"Our power is on, and the furniture came," Mary said. "The phone company was here, too." She handed Alex a piece of paper. "Here's our new number; Gramma thought you should have it."

Alex told Mary about the kitten.

"We have kitten formula and doll bottles," Mary said, "for when Gramma has foster kittens. If your kitty hasn't been weaned yet, let me know, and you can have what you need to feed her."

"Thanks. She looks big enough to eat out of a dish. She's about the size Pete was when we got him."

"Be sure to give her a dish of her own," Mary advised. "Pete will accept her more quickly if he doesn't have to share his food."

"Rocky's the one whose house got burglarized this morning," Alex said.

"Have they found out who did it yet?" Mary asked.

"Not yet," Rocky said. "Sheriff Alvored says we may

never get our things back. There are thousands of burglaries every year, and only a small percent of the items are ever recovered."

After Mary left, Alex found a small bowl for Lizzy and put it on the other side of the kitchen, away from Pete's dish. He didn't put food in it, in case Lizzy needed a different kind of food than what Pete ate.

Soon Benjie burst into the house carrying the cardboard box. Alex could tell from the expression on his brother's face that the kitten was healthy.

Benjie set the box on the floor and opened it. Lizzy scrambled out.

"She's fine," Mrs. Kendrill said. "She got her first shots, and she got wormed. She's supposed to go back in a month. Dr. Rice says she's a tabby cat, one of the most common kind."

"She's about seven weeks old," Benjie said, "and she matches!"

"Matches?" Rocky asked.

Benjie pointed to Lizzy's face, and then to her chest. "Dr. Rice showed me. Her left side is exactly the same as her right side, as if one half of her was a color copy of the other. See? All the stripes and the fur colors match perfectly."

Alex saw that it was true. "She's a copycat," he said.

Benjie laughed.

"How much did it cost?" Mr. Kendrill asked.

"Twenty-nine dollars," Mrs. Kendrill said, "including a bag of kitten food. I wrote a check."

"Typical free cat," Mr. Kendrill said. "Costs money right away."

"She'll be worth it," Benjie said. "Lizzy's the best cat in the whole . . ." He hesitated, looking at Pete. Then he said, "Lizzy's the best girl cat in the whole world."

Alex looked closer at Lizzy's symmetrical patterns. She may be a common tabby cat, he thought, but Benjie was right: her markings were beautiful.

Benjie took Lizzy to bed with him, but after he fell asleep, the kitten went downstairs and sat on Mr. Kendrill's lap.

Alex and Rocky were watching a movie. Alex nudged Rocky with his elbow, then nodded at his dad, who was petting Lizzy and smiling at her. The two boys grinned at each other.

Later that night Lizzy curled up on the rug next to Pete, nuzzled her face up under his front leg, and purred. Her front claws kneaded in and out on Pete's fur.

"Isn't that sweet?" Mrs. Kendrill said, before she and Mr. Kendrill went to bed. "She thinks Pete is her mother."

How embarrassing, thought Pete, but he lay still until Lizzy went to sleep. Then he eased away from her and began his nightly rounds. As the night watchcat he had to stay alert, especially with what had gone on in the neighborhood recently.

5

Pete crouched on Alex's window ledge with his
nose to the screen, glad that Alex liked fresh air at night
even in winter. Pete inhaled deeply as he peered through the
dark trees toward the house next door. His fur rose along
the ridge of his back. He smelled fear, sharp animal fear,
although he couldn't tell what kind of animal was in danger.

Something was wrong at Mary's house.

Pete stepped down to the bed, walked across Alex, who
stirred and turned over, and jumped to the floor. He walked
along the edge of Rocky's sleeping bag, then trotted downstairs to the living-room window. It was closer to Mary's
house, but he could see only the trees and shrubs that were
between the two properties.

He raced back upstairs to his first viewpoint. A van stood
in the neighbor's driveway, its rear door open.

As Pete watched, a figure hurried to the van and placed a
large object inside. Pete tried to slide the window open farther, but it held fast. Frustrated, he pawed at the window.

The figure returned to the house and came back a few seconds later carrying another object. It's the burglar, Pete realized. He's stealing things out of Mary's house!

Pete squinted, trying to get a better look, but the person went back inside. A gray animal about the size of a football came out the door. It had a heart-shaped face, small ears, and dainty pink paws. When it turned, its long skinny tail made it look like a rat from the back side.

That must be Pearly, Pete thought. Mary's possum was loose! He watched as Pearly waddled away from the house, toward the trees.

Pete leaped on top of Alex.

"Oooff!" Alex said. "Get off me, Pete. I was sound asleep."

"Get up," Pete said. "There's trouble next door."

"I fed you before I went to bed," Alex said. "If you ate it all at once, you'll have to wait until morning for more."

"Look out the window," Pete said. "The burglar is taking things out of Mary's house, and he let Pearly out."

Alex groggily rubbed his hands across his eyes, then reached for the small clock on his nightstand. "It's two o'clock in the morning," he said. "I'm going to shut you in the laundry room at night if you act like this."

Pete leaped to the window ledge and pawed frantically at the glass. "Look!" he said. "The van is still there."

"What's the matter with Pete?" Rocky said. "Is he sick?"

"I think he's trying to catch a fly," Alex said. He clicked on the bedside lamp, then sat up and looked at the window. "I don't see any fly," he said.

"*You're wasting time,*" Pete said. "*The possum is out there alone, headed for the woods.*"

"He seems excited," Rocky said.

"As long as I'm awake, I suppose I may as well feed him," Alex said. "I can see we won't get any sleep until I do."

Alex plodded down the stairs, but Pete didn't follow.

When Alex reached the bottom, he looked back. "Come on, Pete," Alex said. "Are you hungry or not?"

"*You can't see anything from down there,*" Pete said. He *dashed back into Alex's bedroom.*

Wearily, Alex climbed the stairs. He kneeled on his bed and started to lift Pete off the window ledge. "You lost your chance to get fed," he said.

Just then he heard a sound from outside, like a car door closing. Apprehension slid down Alex's arms. He turned off the light and looked out. Mary's house was dark.

"Rocky," he whispered, "I heard something from next door."

Still holding Pete, Alex pushed the window farther open.

Rocky stood beside Alex. "I hear it, too," he said. "Someone just started a car, but they haven't turned the lights on."

"Burglars?" Alex set Pete on the bed. "Hurry," he told Rocky. "Maybe we can get out to the street before the car goes past and see who it is."

The two boys raced down the stairs, out the front door, and ran down Alex's driveway. They were not yet to the street when a maroon-colored van passed through the pool of light from the streetlamp.

Two people sat in the front seats, but it was too dark to tell if they were men or women. The boys watched the van continue toward the corner, where the headlights finally came on.

"That van came out of Mary's driveway," Alex said.

"We need to tell your parents," Rocky said. "The sheriff said we should report anything that seems unusual."

The boys went back inside, locking the door behind them.

"Did you see them?" Pete asked. *"Do you know what the burglars look like?"*

Rocky started up the stairs.

"I'll be up as soon as I feed Pete," Alex said. He went to the kitchen and saw that the cat bowl was still half-full.

"You saw something, didn't you?" Alex whispered, holding Pete close to his chest. "Was it that van? You saw that van and you wanted me to see it, too."

"I saw Pearly, too. Pearly got away and went into the trees."

"You're a smart cat, Pete," Alex said.

Pete purred softly, butting his head under Alex's chin. Alex set him down beside his dish.

Pete bit into a cat crunchie. He had done what he could to alert the humans; now he might as well have a little snack.

Alex climbed the stairs and went to the doorway of his parents' bedroom. "Mom?" he said softly. "Dad?"

"What is it, son?" his dad asked.

"I'm sorry to wake you up, but Rocky and I heard a van in the Sunburgs' driveway, and then it drove away without any lights on."

Mrs. Kendrill turned on a lamp.

"We couldn't tell who was in it. It seemed odd that a car would be there this late and that the driver didn't turn his headlights on until he got to the corner."

"Maybe Mrs. Sunburg had a visitor who stayed late," Mr. Kendrill said.

"I didn't see any lights on in the house, and Mary told me she and her grandma were tired and planned to go to bed early."

Alex's parents got out of bed and put on robes. They hurried to Alex's window, and everyone looked toward the neighbors' house. It remained dark.

Pete quit eating and joined them.

"Do you think I should call Mary?" Alex said.

"Yes," Pete said. "Call her so she'll get up and discover that Pearly's gone."

The humans continued to look out the window. Pete's

whiskers quivered impatiently. Cats don't waste time think-ing things over. They act. Humans can't seem to learn that.

"I'd hate to jar them out of a sound sleep over noth-ing," Mr. Kendrill said. "A car driving away from their house doesn't necessarily mean there's a problem."

"Yes, it does," Pete said. "Someone took things from their house and put them in the van."

"Alex," Mrs. Kendrill said, "will you please feed that cat? I can't think when he howls like that."

Alex knew Pete didn't need food, so he picked the cat up and stroked him to keep him quiet.

"When the sheriff was at my house, he said we should report anything at all that seems odd," Rocky said.

"If you don't call," Mr. Kendrill said, "we'll all lie in bed worrying that we should have. I'm sure Mrs. Sunburg and Mary won't mind being awakened when they learn why you called."

Alex dialed the number. After three rings, Mrs. Sunburg answered.

"This is Alex from next door. Is everything all right? I saw a van pull away from your house with its lights off. Mom and Dad thought I'd better call." He covered the mouthpiece with his hand and said, "She's going to look around."

Seconds later, Mrs. Sunburg came back on the line, sounding breathless. "We've been burglarized," she said.

"The sliding-glass patio door was jimmied open and the TV is gone and my antique clock and I don't know what else. I'll call you back after I call the police."

Alex relayed the news.

"Pearly's gone, too," Pete said. *"Tell her to look for Pearly."*

"I think I should go over there," Mrs. Kendrill said. "Mrs. Sunburg doesn't know anyone else in this area yet, and she'll be upset. Alex and Rocky, get dressed and come with me. Mary will need a friend, too."

"I'll stay here in case Benjie wakes up," Mr. Kendrill said. "Call if you need me."

The boys pulled on jeans and sweatshirts, then followed Mrs. Kendrill across the grass to the neighbors' house.

"Don't touch anything," Mrs. Kendrill warned. "The police may want to check for fingerprints."

Mrs. Sunburg let them in. Rufus stood beside her, wagging his tail and acting pleased to have unexpected company.

"Didn't Rufus bark?" Alex asked.

"Rufus sleeps with me," Mary said, "and I had the bedroom door closed. He must not have heard the burglar."

Mary led Alex and Rocky toward the family room to show them the door that had been jimmied opened. "Pearly probably knows what the burglars look like," she said. "I put her cage facing a window at night because pos-sums are nocturnal, and I thought she'd like to look out after dark. She was right there next to the patio door, watching them pry it open." She pointed to Pearly's cage.

"Pearly is a possum," Alex told Rocky.

Mary flicked on the yard light and peered into the yard.

"Too bad Pearly can't talk," Alex said as he lifted the blanket that was draped over the back of the cage. He froze. "Mary," he said, "is the cage door supposed to be open?"

Mary gasped, then dropped to her knees. She flung the blanket aside and peered into the cage.

"Gramma!" she called, her eyes puddling with tears. "Pearly's gone! They stole Pearly!"

"Oh, no," Alex said. He and Rocky knelt on the floor beside Mary and looked into the empty possum cage.

Mrs. Sunburg rushed into the room, followed by Mrs. Kendrill.

"Are you sure?" Mrs. Sunburg said. "She isn't hiding in her hollow log?"

"Her cage door is open," Mary said, "and she's gone."

"Why would a thief steal a possum?" Mrs. Kendrill asked. "Surely there isn't much value."

"Only sentimental value," Mrs. Sunburg said sadly.

"Probably the burglar thought Pearly was a rare exotic animal," Rocky said, "like an ocelot or something he could sell for a lot of money."

"I'm surprised Pearly didn't bite whoever it was," Mary said. "Possums have a lot of teeth, and we've been careful not to socialize Pearly so that she can be released."

"Maybe she did bite him," Alex said. "Maybe the thief picked her up and she bit him, and the thief dropped her, and Pearly's hiding somewhere."

Rocky looked carefully at the floor near the cage. "I don't see any blood," he said.

Alex said, "The burglar might have opened the cage, and then when he saw that Pearly was only a possum—" He stopped when he saw the look on Mary's face. "I mean, when he saw that it might be hard to find a buyer for Pearly, he didn't bother to latch the cage again."

"Or maybe the thief opened the cage just to be mean," Mrs. Sunburg said. "I hate to say it, but there are people who don't care about animals." She reached down to pat Rufus, who was now sniffing all around Pearly's cage. "Rufus is proof of that."

Alex's stomach twisted into a knot. He didn't like to think about people who would shoot at a dog or purposely let an injured animal out of its cage, but he knew such people existed.

Mary peered under the couch. "Not here," she said.

"I'll help you look," Alex said.

"So will I," Rocky said.

While the adults discussed the burglary and waited for the sheriff to arrive, Alex, Mary, and Rocky looked under the beds, examined the inside of every closet, and checked beneath all the furniture. There were still stacks of unopened cardboard cartons piled everywhere, so it took a while to look everyplace that a possum might hide.

"She must be outside," Mary said. "The burglar left the door open. Pearly probably smelled the fresh air and went toward it. She would want to be outdoors, especially after dark. I hope there aren't any coyotes around here or . . ." Mary couldn't finish the sentence. Tears choked the words away.

"Do you have flashlights?" Rocky asked.

"We haven't unpacked them yet. I don't even know which box they're in."

"I'll go get flashlights from my house," Alex said. "I'll be right back."

Alex dashed home. His dad was in the kitchen, making hot chocolate.

"The burglar let Mary's possum out," Alex said as he got a flashlight from the kitchen cupboard. "Rocky and I are going to help her look for it." He found two more flashlights in the closet next to the front door.

"She really has a possum?" Mr. Kendrill said. "I thought that was one of Benjie's stories."

"She has one temporarily," Alex said. "At least she does if we can find it. It's recovering from an injury and isn't ready to survive on its own."

52

"I'll come with you," Pete said. He walked to the back door. "I can see in the dark, and I know what Pearly smells like because I smelled her on Mary's hand."

"Don't go beyond our yard and Mary's," Mr. Kendrill said. "I don't want you boys wandering around the whole neighborhood at this time of night."

"We won't," Alex said. "One of Pearly's paws was injured, so she doesn't move real fast. We think she headed for the trees."

"I know which way she went," Pete said. "I'll show you." He stuck his nose in the crack of the door, waiting for Alex to open it.

"Get back, Pete," Alex said, putting his hand against Pete's chest and giving him a gentle nudge.

Pete's ears flattened as Alex pushed him away from the door.

Alex turned the doorknob.

Pete crouched.

When the door opened and Alex stepped out, Pete leaped over Alex's foot and hit the porch running.

"Pete!" Alex yelled. "Come back here!"

Pete ran straight toward where he had seen Pearly. "This way!" he said. "Follow me!"

Alex, still holding the door open, turned back to his dad. "Pete ran out," he said. "I tried to keep him in, but he jumped past me."

"We should have named that cat Houdini," Mr. Kendrill said. "He vanishes every chance he gets."

"I'll try to catch him," Alex said.

"I'll call him, too," Mr. Kendrill said. "Not that it will do any good. We know from long experience that Pete comes home when Pete is good and ready, and not before."

Alex shined his light across the yard, but Pete had already disappeared.

6

Mary and Rocky met Alex outside Mary's house. Mary held a pet carrier by the handle. Alex gave his friends each a flashlight.

"If we see Pearly, we'll try to get her in the carrier," Mary said. "She'll be scared, so be careful."

"Could she survive if we don't catch her?" Rocky asked.

"Her foot is nearly healed, but a housing development isn't the place to release her. She needs to go in the woods."

"Pete's out, too," Alex told her. "He leaped right over my foot when I opened the door."

"I'm sorry," Mary said. "You're trying to help me, and your pet gets loose."

"Pete's escaped before," Alex said, "though not at night. We used to let him go outside during the daytime, before we knew how dangerous that can be. Now he's an indoor cat. I still take him for walks on his leash, so he knows the neighborhood and can find his way home."

Alex tried to sound as if he wasn't worried about Pete, but it made him anxious to have Pete out by himself, especially tonight. So many bad things had happened lately.

As they talked, the kids walked slowly around Mary's house, shining their flashlights back and forth on the grass.

"Pearly might have headed for the trees," Mary said. "Possums have a prehensile tail, you know."

"A what tail?" said Rocky.

"Prehensile. That means they can grasp with it and can use it to help themselves climb trees. They can even hang by their tails."

"No kidding," Alex said. "Have you ever seen Pearly do that?"

"She's never been up a tree since she's been with us. We've only been taking care of her for a week."

Alex wished he had grabbed his jacket. December nights are cold, and the wind was starting to blow.

They walked slowly, shining the lights into clumps of tall grass and bushes.

As they approached the wooded area that connected their backyards, Alex heard a familiar sound from deep in the trees.

"Over here," Pete said. "I can smell her! Pearly came this way."

"Is that Pete?" Rocky asked.

"Yes," Alex said.

"Go ahead and catch him and take him home," Mary said. "Rocky and I can keep looking for Pearly."

Alex hesitated, debating whether to say what he was thinking. Lately he had begun to suspect that Pete was not an ordinary cat. He wondered if Pete understood what people said and even tried to communicate with them.

Alex had not mentioned this suspicion to anyone. He was afraid his parents would react the way they did when Benjie told his fanciful stories about flying animals.

Tonight Rocky had witnessed Pete's behavior. He knew that the reason the boys had seen the van was that Pete woke Alex up, as if the cat had wanted him to look out the window.

Alex decided to take a chance. "I hope you won't think this is a really far-out thing to say," he began, "but Pete sometimes seems to know things. He acts like he understands what's going on as if he were human. The reason we saw that van tonight was because Pete jumped on me while I was asleep, and meowed until I got up to feed him, and then he ran to the window, and when we looked out, we saw the van leaving. It was as if he knew it was there and was trying to show us."

"That's true," Rocky said. "Pete acted strange."

"Cats are very intelligent," Mary said.

"Hurry up!" Pete called. "Pearly's smell is strong right at the base of this maple tree."

"I'm wondering if he might be calling us to come now," Alex said. "Maybe he knows where Pearly is. Let's skip this part of the yard and go over where Pete is."

"Don't stand there talking. Get a move on!"

Alex started into the wooded area at the rear of the Kendrills' property. Mary and Rocky followed. Besides shining their lights back and forth on the ground, they also aimed the lights up into the branches of each tree that they passed. They couldn't see Pete yet, but they could certainly hear him.

"I smell her! I smell her! Come this way!"

"If he's found Pearly, he's probably scaring her half to death with all that screeching," Mary said. "I don't imagine Pearly has ever seen a cat—certainly not one as big as Pete."

Alex's flashlight picked up two gleaming eyes. "There he is," he said. He kept the light aimed at Pete. The cat stood beside the brush pile where Alex and his dad had heaped branches that had come down in a recent windstorm.

"Birds and small animals need brush piles for cover," Mr. Kendrill had told Alex. "Eventually the branches will rot and enrich the soil, so why cart them off to the dump?"

Mary swept her light across the tangled tree limbs.

"I tracked her this far," Pete said. *"The smell goes into these branches, but it doesn't come out the other side. She's hiding in the branches."*

"Can you make him be quiet?" Mary asked. "Pearly's scared of every little unexpected sound, and I imagine an animal noise is the most frightening of all. If she is hiding in there, she'll never come out while Pete's meowing."

"I'm only trying to help," Pete said.

"Be quiet, Pete," Alex said. He inched closer to the cat.

Rocky walked to the far side of the brush pile and moved his flashlight across the branches. "I don't see Pearly," he whispered.

"She's in there, all right," Pete said.

"Shh," Alex said.

Mary crouched on the ground, beside Pete. Both of them peered into the brush pile as Alex moved closer. Mary slid her hand over to Pete. "I have hold of his collar," she said.

"Traitor!" Pete said. "I thought you wanted to pet me."

Alex picked up Pete. "I'm going to put Pete in the house," Alex said. "I'll be right back."

"Is this the thanks I get for helping?" Pete said. "Put me down!"

As Alex carried a struggling Pete out of the trees and across the grass, he heard voices. The police had arrived at Mary's house. He hoped they would catch the burglars soon.

Alex had planned to open the door, dump Pete inside, and return to Mary and Rocky, but when he opened the door, he saw Benjie sitting at the kitchen table, sobbing. The knot in Alex's stomach tightened.

"He woke up," Mr. Kendrill said. "I told him what happened."

"If the bad guys stole Pearly, they might come and steal Lizzy, too," Benjie said, "or Pete. Or one of us."

"Pete's right here," Alex said. "He's fine. I brought him home."

"Nobody's going to steal Lizzy or Pete," Mr. Kendrill said. "Burglars steal things they can sell. There are 'free kitten' ads in the paper all the time."

"The police are at Mary's house," Alex said, hoping that would make Benjie feel safer.

Benjie didn't answer. He wiped his nose on his pajama sleeve and cried harder.

"I need to go back and help Mary and Rocky," Alex said. "We think Pearly is hiding in our brush pile."

"She is," Pete said. "I could smell her."

"Be careful," Mr. Kendrill said. "That possum is a wild animal, and it's probably scared."

"Mary has a pet carrier like Pete's to put Pearly in when we find her."

Pete ran to the door and got ready to bolt, but this time Mr. Kendrill held Pete while Alex went out.

"This is an outrage," Pete said as he tried to wiggle out of Mr. Kendrill's grasp. "I'm the one who found Pearly; I should get to see her."

60

As Alex hurried back toward the trees, he felt angry and frustrated. Those burglars had no right to break into houses and steal things and let animals loose and frighten little kids.

Until today, when there was news of any crime, Benjie had wanted to grab his spy kit and go hunt for the bad guys. Now Benjie was scared. He had cried when he heard about the burglary at Rocky's house, and he had been watching for criminals rather than flying green panthers when he found Lizzy. These break-ins had been too close to home.

Alex hurried toward the brush pile.

"I think I see her," Mary said. "While you were gone, we could hear rustling right about there." She pointed to the center of the brush pile. "We waited for you to get back so that the two of you can guide her into the cage while I hold it open."

"Let's take the branches off the top and work our way down into the center," Rocky suggested.

"I'll go on the other side," Alex said. "We can prop our flashlights on the ground so they're aimed where we're working."

Alex went to the far side of the brush pile. He put the handle end of his flashlight on the ground and stuck a small stone under the wide end to aim the light toward the center of the pile. Mary did the same on her side, and Rocky aimed his light at one end of the pile.

They began pulling branches from the top of the heap, and tossing them aside.

"I hope we aren't destroying any bird nests," Mary said. She tugged at a large branch whose twigs were twined with the branch beneath it like clasped fingers.

"The police are at your house," Alex said.

"They don't need to talk to me," Mary said. "Gramma knows as much about what happened as I do."

They pulled more branches off the pile. "We should have worn gloves," Rocky said. "We're getting all scratched and cut."

"Maybe we shouldn't say anything," Mary whispered.

Alex and Rocky nodded agreement.

A light rain began to fall. Alex shivered as a raindrop hit the back of his neck. He heard rustling in the brush pile and saw Mary move the carrier closer.

Alex peered down through the branches toward the sound. He saw a patch of gray fur. He waved to get Mary's attention, then pointed. Rocky pointed, too.

Mary pulled two more branches off the pile.

Alex looked down at a triangular-shaped white face with a pink nose and small dark ears. He had never seen a live possum. The rest of the fur looked light where it was close to the body and silver-gray at the edge.

She had whiskers, much like Pete's. Not counting her tail, Pearly was about a foot long. Her pink feet scrabbled in the leaves as she tried to burrow into the brush pile.

Mary grabbed the pet carrier and held the open door toward Pearly.

Alex clapped his hands and shouted, "Run, Pearly!"

The startled possum turned back toward Mary and waddled out of the brush pile. Mary positioned the carrier so that Pearly went straight into it.

"I got her!" she cried as she latched the carrier door shut.

"Is she okay?" Rocky asked.

Mary shined her flashlight into the cage. "She looks fine. Let's take her home."

"I'll come back tomorrow and put the brush pile back together," Alex said.

"I'll help," Mary said. "Thanks for coming with me to find Pearly. I don't think I could have caught her by myself."

"I'm glad we found her," Alex said.

The boys went to Mary's house, where Alex and Rocky answered questions from the sheriff about the van. They told exactly what they had seen, which didn't seem like much.

"How did you happen to look out the window at two in the morning?" Mrs. Sunburg asked.

"My cat woke me up," Alex said. He looked at Rocky and Mary, who both nodded as if to say they knew Pete had awakened Alex because of the van, but they weren't going to say that.

When the sheriff left, Alex, his mom, and Rocky ran through the rain to Alex's house. Mr. Kendrill had hot chocolate ready for them.

Benjie had stopped crying and was petting Lizzy. "Did you find Pearly?" he asked.

"Yes. She's back in her cage."

"Thanks to me," said Pete.

"I'm going to bed," Mr. Kendrill said.

"So am I," Alex said.

"Me, too," said Rocky. The boys finished their hot chocolate and rinsed their cups.

"I'm going to stay up and play with Lizzy," Benjie said.

"You are going to bed," Mrs. Kendrill said.

"Lizzy wants to play."

"You can take Lizzy upstairs with you, but leave your door open so she can get out if she wants to."

"She won't want to," Benjie said as he carried the kitten up the stairs. "She needs me to protect her if the burglars come here and try to steal her."

Alex noticed that his parents didn't try to convince Benjie that this wasn't possible.

Alex flopped into bed, and Rocky crawled back into the sleeping bag. Tired to the core, they lay listening to the rain on the roof.

"It's raining hard now," Rocky said. "I'm glad Pearly and Pete are both safely inside where they belong."

Alex was glad of that, too, but he couldn't relax and fall asleep. Even after he heard Rocky's soft, even breathing, Alex thought about the burglaries, and about Benjie. He heard the grandfather clock downstairs strike four, then five. The knot in his stomach didn't go away.

First Rocky's house and now Mary's. What was next?

7

The next morning after Rocky left, Alex started into the bathroom. He stopped when he saw his brother. Benjie was so absorbed in what he was doing, he didn't notice Alex watching him.

Benjie had six envelopes lined up on the bathroom counter. He had printed on them in black marker, with a single word on each envelope: MOM DAD ALEX BENJIE PETE LIZZY.

Benjie ran a comb through Mom's hairbrush, removed the loose hair, and stuffed it into the envelope that had her name on it.

"What are you doing?" Alex asked.

"I'm collecting DNA."

"What?"

"DNA. The police can identify people that way. It's like a fingerprint, only better. I read about it in one of my spy books. They can tell from a bit of skin or blood or hair which person it came from."

"I know what DNA is," Alex said. "Why are you collecting it?"

"I'm getting some DNA from everybody in our family," Benjie said, "in case the burglar kidnaps one of us. Then the police can check the clothes of any suspects for hair or blood or skin, and if the DNA matches, they can prove he did it and that will help find the kidnapped person."

Using tape, Benjie carefully sealed the envelope marked MOM. Then he returned the hairbrush to its drawer.

"The burglar isn't going to kidnap any of us," Alex said. It made him sad that Benjie was so worried. Although Benjie already knew how to read well, he was only seven years old; he should be outside riding his bike or looking for one of his imaginary flying animals. He shouldn't be gathering evidence to trap a possible kidnapper.

"How do you know he won't kidnap us?" Benjie said. "He's a bad guy, isn't he? Bad guys do lots of terrible things."

"The burglar only takes items he can sell," Alex said. "He steals television sets, cameras, jewelry—stuff that he can get rid of in a hurry to raise some cash." Alex tried to make a joke of the situation. "He won't kidnap one of us because who would pay the ransom? Mom and Dad are always complaining that they're short of money."

Benjie took an electric razor out of the cupboard. He opened the DAD envelope, held the head of the razor inside, then tapped it against the side of the sink.

"I'd pay," Benjie said. "I'd give my allowance and everything in my piggy bank and all my birthday money to get you or Lizzy or Pete or Mom or Dad back."

Fondness for his little brother filled Alex. Benjie could be a real pain sometimes, but down deep he was a good kid.

"Hey, I'd pay for you, too," Alex said, "but it won't be necessary."

"Do you have a hairbrush?" Benjie asked, after he taped the DAD envelope shut.

"No, but you can empty my razor."

Benjie gave him a disgusted look. "You don't shave yet."

"I was kidding. I don't have a hairbrush, either. I use a comb."

"Would you comb your hair and give me what comes out?"

Alex sighed. He could tell he'd never convince Benjie that his DNA project was unnecessary. Once his brother got started on a spy activity, there was no stopping him.

"If you don't want to comb your hair," Benjie said, "you could prick your finger and let me have the blood."

"No way." Alex ran a comb through his hair several times. Maybe this is a good thing, he thought. If it eases Benjie's anxiety to feel prepared for a disaster, then let him go ahead and collect DNA.

Benjie held the ALEX envelope open while Alex cleaned the comb into it.

"Thanks," Benjie said. "If you hadn't come along, I was going to swipe your toothbrush. There's DNA on a toothbrush, too."

"I'm glad you didn't do that. I'd hate to have you carrying my old used toothbrush around in your spy kit. It would probably get moldy."

Benjie finally smiled. "Now all I have to do is brush Pete," he said as he put five sealed envelopes into his spy backpack. "I already did Lizzy, but Pete ran away."

"Good luck getting him to hold still for the brush. I never can." Alex didn't point out that burglars were unlikely to steal Pete under any circumstances. For one thing, they'd never catch him. Pete disliked strangers and usually hid until he was sure of their intentions. Also, Pete was not an expensive purebred; he was a mixed breed of unknown background whom Alex had adopted at the humane society—hardly a target for kidnappers.

Benjie carried his backpack out of the bathroom.

"Forget it," said Pete as Benjie approached him with the cat brush in one hand and an envelope in the other. Pete leaped to the top of the piano.

"Get down, Pete," Benjie said. "I need some of your fur for a DNA sample, in case the burglar kidnaps you."

"Ha!" said Pete. "Let that burglar lay a hand on me, and the only DNA samples you'll find will be HIS skin." He crouched on the back corner of the piano, out of Benjie's reach.

Benjie stood on the piano bench. Pete tried to jump down, but Benjie grabbed his collar and hung on with his left hand while he ran the brush across Pete's back with his right hand.

Pete growled. He was tempted to give Benjie a scratch on the hand to teach him a lesson, but he restrained himself. Benjie was usually good to Pete, and Pete believed it was wrong to hurt someone except in self-protection. He didn't like to be brushed, but he knew he would survive it. He held still and let Benjie finish.

After two swipes with the brush, Benjie let go of Pete's collar. He carefully removed Pete's fur from the brush.

"Thanks, Pete," he said. "This might save your life someday if the cat burglar comes here."

Pete watched as Benjie put the fur in an envelope and taped the envelope shut, then put it in his spy backpack.

As soon as Benjie left, Pete jumped down from the piano. He licked his shoulder vigorously to remove any trace of the hated cat brush. Then he walked to the kitchen for a second breakfast. Being brushed, even briefly, gave him a craving for crunchies.

After he ate, Pete went into Alex's room and read the titles of the books on Alex's desk. When he found the book he was looking for, he placed his paw on the spine and pulled. He had to tug three times before the fat red dictionary finally tumbled to the floor.

Pete turned the pages until he came to the word he

wanted: "cat." He had decided to improve his family's vocabulary. The only words he ever heard them say that began with "cat" were insulting.

"Cat burglar" was the worst. No real cat would ever break into a house and steal what didn't belong to him, but the news announcers on TV said cat burglar all the time when they talked about a thief. Even his own people had called the person who had stolen Mary's computer a cat burglar because the robber had come noiselessly in the night.

"Catnap" was another overused term. It implied that cats are lazy animals, forever catching a few winks of sleep here and there. While it was true that Pete liked a cozy bed as well as the next creature, no cat has ever been lazy.

Yesterday Mrs. Kendrill had said "catastrophe" when she told about the problems at her friend's house. Pete had heard that word before. Whenever something really bad happened, people said it was a catastrophe. Nobody ever talked about a birdastrophe or a cowastrophe or a humanastrophe.

Why were cats blamed for everything? Humans get themselves into far worse messes than cats do. Cats don't start wars or drop bombs on one another or hijack airplanes. Cats know it's important to help other creatures, even when they're different than we are. Many humans hadn't learned that yet.

There must be other, better cat words, Pete thought, and it was time to find out what they were.

His eyes scanned the page of the dictionary after the word

"cat." Some words were long and hard to pronounce. Others had such complicated meanings that Pete would never be able to work them into an ordinary conversation.

He was pleased to find "cat's eye" and learn that it referred to various gems, but dismayed to discover that "cat-tail" was defined only as a plant. Pete's own dark tail was both handsome and useful—certainly worth as much of a mention as a plant. Of course, humans had written the dictionary, so it was bound to be slanted in their favor.

Finally Pete found exactly the sort of word he had hoped for—"catapult: a device for launching an airplane at flying speed, as from an aircraft carrier." Pete read on. The second definition made the word even better. "To throw or launch as if by a catapult."

Pete trotted downstairs and into the family room. His people had finished breakfast, and Mr. and Mrs. Kendrill were watching the news on TV. Alex was clearing the table. Benjie was trying to sneak cookies out of the cookie jar and put them in his backpack without his mother hearing the jar lid clink. Lizzy was asleep.

Ordinarily Pete would have chosen a time like this to have a cat fit. Today he planned something even better.

Pete crouched on the floor. His tail flopped back and forth. "Watch this!" he yelled. His hind feet gave a mighty shove and he leaped to the top of the piano. "Did you see me?" Pete said. "I catapulted! I am a catapulting cat!"

No one paid any attention to him, so Pete jumped down. Next he crouched in front of the entertainment center, which was considerably higher than the piano. The television set was in the middle, with bookshelves on both sides and above it and cupboards below.

"Look at this!" Pete shrieked, and he flew past the television screen to the top of the bookshelf.

"Mercy!" Mrs. Kendrill said. "Did you see that? Pete jumped up there as if he'd been shot from a cannon."

"*I catapulted!*" Pete said. "*I launched myself at flying speed!*"

"Wow!" said Benjie. "Look what Pete did!"

"Maybe he has worms," Mr. Kendrill said. "Is he due for his checkup at the vet?"

Pete growled. Not the vet! "I won't go," he said. "*You'll never catch me.*" He catapulted to the floor, raced across the family room, and ran up the stairs. He would practice his catapulting in Alex's bedroom, where his behavior could not be misinterpreted.

"You'd better catch him, Alex," Mrs. Kendrill said, "before he tears the house apart. Perhaps there's a splinter in his paw."

"I don't think there's anything wrong with him," Alex said. "He's having a cat fit because he's bored."

"Maybe he saw a flying green panther out the window," Benjie said, "and he's trying to warn us." He went to the

73

window and peered out. "I think I hear one," he whispered. "It's probably landing on our roof."

Lizzy, awakened by Pete's hollering, raced into the family room, jumped on the couch, ran across Mr. Kendrill's lap, slid down his pant leg, and climbed halfway up the drapes. "Mrowr," she said as she clung to the fabric.

"Get down, Lizzy," Mrs. Kendrill said. "No, no."

Mr. Kendrill clicked off the television. "This house is a zoo," he said.

"The news is too depressing to watch anyway," Mrs. Kendrill said.

"Was there another burglary?" Benjie asked.

"I wouldn't know," Mr. Kendrill said. "With all the commotion going on, I couldn't hear a word."

"There weren't any more burglaries," Alex said as he started up the stairs to check on Pete.

"I think Pete's giving Lizzy lessons in how to have a cat fit," Benjie said. "This morning they both ran across my bed. That's what woke me up so early."

"I knew it was a mistake to keep that kitten," Mr. Kendrill said. "All we need is two of them screeching and racing through the house."

"We can't take her back," Benjie said. "We don't know where she came from."

"We aren't taking Lizzy anywhere," Mrs. Kendrill said. She had plucked the kitten from the drapery and was petting her. "She'll calm down when she gets older."

"Don't hold your breath," Mr. Kendrill said. "Pete seems to think the family room is a trampoline."

"It's supposed to rain this afternoon, Benjie," Mrs. Kendrill said, "so if you want to play outside today, you'd better do it now."

"I'm going to my spy hideout," Benjie said as he collected his binoculars and his backpack.

"If you see anyone drop off a box," Mr. Kendrill said, "leave it there."

Benjie didn't see any more boxes. He didn't find any more kittens. He didn't even see a flying green panther. Of course, he wasn't looking for panthers now, he was looking for burglars. He was the only spy on his block; it was up to him to watch for anything suspicious.

The next morning at breakfast Mrs. Kendrill said, "Remember, Benjie, this is an early dismissal day for you because of conferences, so I won't be here when you get home from school. You're to go to Mrs. Sunburg's house until Alex or I come for you. She likes little boys and says she's happy to have you anytime I can't be here after school."

"Okay," Benjie said. "I'll play with Rufus."

Alex was glad to hear his brother say that. Benjie had spent most of yesterday watching the street with his binoculars. When Lizzy was awake, he played with her, but kittens sleep a lot, and Benjie had spent the rest of his time looking for "bad guys."

When Benjie had first started pretending to be a spy, his family had encouraged him. Benjie was an imaginative child, and the spy games gave him a way to playact. But since the burglaries, Benjie's pretending had solemn undertones of fear. It wasn't a game for Benjie anymore, Alex thought. It was real.

Alex had overheard his parents discussing Benjie and knew they were concerned about him, too. Last night Benjie had awakened in the night crying from a nightmare, and when his parents asked him about the dream, he had said, "The bad guys came and stole Pete and Lizzy."

"The bad guys would never do that," Dad had said, but Alex knew Benjie was unconvinced.

This morning, Benjie had his binoculars around his neck while he ate breakfast.

"Spread the jelly with your knife, Benjie," Mrs. Kendrill said, "not with your fingers."

"If Mom isn't home when you get here," Benjie said to Alex, "you should come to Mrs. Sunburg's house, too."

Alex started to say he was old enough to be home by himself, then realized that Benjie was worried about him.

Alex smiled at his brother. "I'll do that," he said.

"Promise?"

"Promise."

Alex grabbed his lunch bag, stuffed it in his backpack, and started for the door. "See you tonight," he called as he dashed for the school bus, which was already rumbling down Elm Lane.

Benjie's bus came an hour later in the mornings than Alex's did. Mrs. Kendrill reminded Benjie, before he got on his own bus, that he was to go to Mrs. Sunburg's house that afternoon. "Go straight there as soon as you get off the bus," she said.

"I will, Mom," he said.

But he didn't.

8

*T*he telephone woke Pete from his afternoon nap. It rang until the answering machine clicked on. Whoever was calling did not leave a message.

Moments later, Pete heard a noise at the front door. He padded into the living room, jumped onto the window ledge, and looked out. A van had backed into the driveway and was parked facing away from the house.

Pete's tail thumped against the wall. Was it the same van that Pete had seen at Mary's house Saturday night? Pete wasn't sure. It had been a dark night, and he had looked at the burglar and Pearly rather than the vehicle, but he thought this one was the same color.

"Mrowr?" said Lizzy, who had followed him into the living room. She reached up and batted at Pete's tail.

It had been a disappointment to discover that Lizzy could not understand what the people said, nor could she speak any language other than Cat. Pete hoped to teach her English, but so far his efforts had been in vain.

"Mrowr," Lizzy repeated, giving Pete's tail another whack.

"Not now," Pete said. He curled his tail around his haunches where the kitten couldn't reach it. "I'll play with you later."

The noise continued at the door. The bell didn't ring and nobody knocked, but Pete heard rubbing sounds coming through the keyhole.

Someone's picking the lock, he realized. The van does belong to the burglars.

The front door opened. Two men walked in, leaving the door open behind them.

Pete sat as still as a stump. He watched the men closely, noticing details of their clothing and looks. Benjie had talked so much about his spy activities that Pete knew exactly what to do. He would be a spy cat. Since the humans were not home, it was up to him to trap the villains. Pete's whiskers twitched with excitement. Spy cat. He rather liked the sound of that.

The tall man in the plaid shirt called out, "Hey, Joanie! We're here!"

The short one with the beard yelled, "Anybody home?"

Joanie? thought Pete. Who's Joanie? Have these men come to the wrong place—or are they pretending to know someone, as a way to make sure that nobody's home? If someone answered their call, they'd probably apologize and leave in a hurry.

Lizzy trotted toward the men.

"Stay away from them," Pete hissed, but his warning was too late.

"Get outta here, cat," said the tall man. He kicked at Lizzy, missing her by only an inch.

The terrified kitten scuttled under the couch.

Pete stayed on the window ledge, trying to decide what to do. There was no one to run to for help; he would have to act on his own.

Maybe I can take something from the truck, Pete thought, an item that would help the police trace the men after they leave. If I could find a piece of mail with a name and address on it, and carry it into the house, it would be a clue for the police to follow.

"We may not have much time," the bearded man said.

"Let's start upstairs." The one in the plaid shirt started toward the stairs.

The bearded man followed.

When Pete could hear both men moving about overhead, he jumped to the floor, trotted to the door, and went out.

The rear door of the van was open. Pete leaped inside.

The back of the van was empty; all the seats except the driver's and front passenger's had been removed. Pete smelled dirt, and grease, and newspaper.

He also smelled french fries and hamburger. Those smells came from the passenger's seat. Pete stepped into the front of the van and hopped on the seat beside a white paper bag.

One french fry, he told himself. Just one, to keep my

strength up, and then I have to get down to business. He tipped the bag over, then dragged a french fry out of its carton onto the seat. He was eating it when the men shoved something into the back of the van. Pete held still and quit chewing. The men went back in the house.

Pete peered into the back of the van and saw the Kendrills' television set. He finished his french fry and began looking for anything that might identify the burglars. There were candy wrappers, an empty chocolate-milk carton, and a few crumpled papers. Pete couldn't smooth out the papers to see what they were.

He lay on the floor and stuck his paw under the passenger's seat. He fished out a receipt from a gas station, but it had been a cash sale. No credit card number and no name.

He went to the driver's seat and put his paw under it. He hauled out an aluminum can, an empty cigarette package, and a filthy knit stocking cap.

The men returned. This time they loaded Alex's bike into the van. Oh, he won't like this, Pete thought. Next they carried out the Kendrills' grandfather clock.

Pete saw the glove compartment and wondered if the men kept any papers in there. He tried to open it, but he couldn't release the latch.

Each time he heard the men coming to the van, he crouched on the floor and waited until they went back inside. Then he kept sniffing on the floor and feeling under the seats.

Once he jumped on the seat, stood on his hind legs, and

pulled the sun visor down, in case the men had stuck some-thing up there that would identify them, but the only thing held up by the visor was a pair of sunglasses, which bonked Pete on the head.

While he waited for his head to quit throbbing, he took a brief break and ate a few more french fries. Why didn't cat-food companies ever make a french-fried-potato flavor? Pete was tired of fish and liver.

He had finished the last french fry when the thieves slid two big boxes into the van. Pete saw that one box contained silverware, the video camera, Alex's Game Boy, and Mrs. Kendrill's portable sewing machine. The other box held the computer keyboard, the VCR, two calculators, and a stack of video movies.

I have to stop them, Pete thought. I can't let them steal my family's favorite things! But what could he do? He was a brave, strong cat, but he was no match for two burly men.

Maybe if he ate the hamburger, it would clear his mind and give him an idea. Pete pulled the hamburger onto the floor and chewed the wrapper open. He hoped the burglar hadn't put pickles inside. Catsup was okay because it began with c-a-t, but Pete never could understand why humans spoiled perfectly good meat by adding pickles.

Benjie remembered that he was supposed to go to Mrs. Sun-burg's house after school. He was looking forward to playing tuggy-toy with Rufus again, as he had on the day Mrs. Sunburg and Mary had moved in. Maybe by now Howley Girl was well enough that he could play with her, too. Also, Mrs. Sunburg had said if she had time she would bake some cookies.

But as he walked past his own driveway on the way to Mrs. Sunburg's house, Benjie saw a van parked at his house. Mom must have gotten home earlier than she thought she would, and now she had company.

The van looked like the one that the Kendrills' carpet had come in when they were building their house. Were Mom and Dad getting carpet for their bedroom? They had said it would be a year or two before they could afford bedroom carpet, but maybe Mom had found a good sale and bought it now. Mom loved buying things on sale. She said getting stuff at half price was almost as good as being rich enough not to care about the price at all.

Benjie looked again. There wasn't any lettering on the side of this van. It must be a friend of Mom's, not a carpet delivery.

Benjie hesitated. He still wanted to play with Rufus, but it would be fun to meet Mom's guest, too. Maybe Mom had stopped at the bakery on her way home and bought a chocolate cake. She did that sometimes, for company. She might be serving chocolate cake right now.

Benjie decided to go home long enough to have a snack. Then he would go visit Mrs. Sunburg and Rufus.

The last time Benjie had arrived home when Mom had

company, he had been scolded later for shouting and banging the door. "Use your indoor voice when we have guests," Mom had told him. "Close the door quietly and say 'Hello, I'm glad to meet you' when you're introduced."

Benjie decided to surprise Mom with his perfect manners. Maybe she'd give him a bigger slice of cake. He angled across the grass and went around the house to the kitchen door, as usual, half expecting that it would be locked. It was not.

Benjie turned the knob and slipped inside.

9

Benjie pulled the kitchen door closed until it clicked. He took off his shoes and left them on the throw rug. Mom didn't like it when he tracked dirt across the floor.

Instead of yelling "I'm home!" as he normally would, Benjie tiptoed across the kitchen. He looked for a white bakery box on the countertop, but he didn't see one. Mom must not have bought a chocolate cake, after all.

He heard footsteps walking around upstairs. Mom and her friend were up there.

Benjie decided he might as well take advantage of being alone. Since there wasn't any cake, he'd eat a few cookies. He could take more when he was by himself than he could if he waited until Mom and her friend came downstairs. Mom always limited him to three.

He lifted the lid of the cookie jar carefully and helped himself to five oatmeal-raisin cookies. Lizzy ran into the room and got into her cat bed. Benjie petted her while he ate two cookies.

While he munched the other cookies he walked through the family room and into the living room.

Benjie stopped. The front door stood wide open. Was Mom's guest leaving? But he still heard footsteps upstairs.

Mom would never let the door stay open this way, because of Pete and Lizzy. Pete was always trying to sneak outside, and everyone in the family was careful to keep him in. Mom's friend must not have closed the door securely when she got here.

Benjie hurried across the room to close the door. He hoped Pete wasn't already outside. Lizzy was in her bed, but now that Benjie thought about it, he realized Pete had not greeted him when he first came in. Usually when the family was gone, Pete ran to them and meowed when they returned, as if welcoming them or complaining that he had been left home alone.

Maybe Pete was upstairs with Mom. When she and her friend came down, Benjie would ask them if Pete was up there.

When Benjie reached the front door, he saw that the back door of the van was open, too. He looked into the van and gasped as if he'd seen a ghost. With his hand on the doorknob and his mouth open in astonishment, he stepped outside and looked more closely.

Inside the van he saw the Kendrills' TV set and their grandfather clock and Alex's bicycle and two boxes full of other things that belonged to Benjie's family.

As Benjie gaped at the van, voices came from the top of the stairs.

"We've got room for one more box," a man said.

"Let's check the kitchen drawers," a different man replied, "and then we'll get out of here."

With a sickening certainty, Benjie knew that Mom wasn't upstairs. She didn't have company. The van belonged to the bad guys.

Footsteps clattered down the stairs.

Benjie's heart hammered so loudly in his chest that he feared the men would hear it. He knew he didn't have much time to get away. Should he run—or should he try to hide?

The bad guys were headed for the kitchen. What if they saw Benjie's shoes on the rug? They might figure out that he was home and come looking for him.

What if they saw Lizzy asleep in her little cat bed and decided to put her in their box and take her away in the van? Maybe that's why Pete had not come to greet Benjie. Maybe the bad guys had already shut Pete in a box and put him in the van.

Fighting back tears, Benjie hesitated on the porch. Brave spies don't run away, he told himself. I need to stay here and get evidence against the bad guys. I need to make sure they don't kidnap Lizzy or Pete.

Mrs. Sunburg put the last pan of snickerdoodles in the oven. She remembered that young boys are always hungry when they get home from school, and they like cookies, especially cookies that are fresh out of the oven.

Mrs. Sunburg felt so fortunate that she and Mary could live in this lovely new house, with plenty of room for her foster animals.

She was lucky to have neighbors who were friendly, too. When Mrs. Kendrill had come over Saturday afternoon with a loaf of banana bread to welcome her to the neighborhood, Mrs. Sunburg had been overjoyed.

The women had shared a pot of tea and Mrs. Sunburg had told how helpful Alex and Benjie had been, carrying in all those boxes. She had offered to have the boys visit anytime.

Mrs. Kendrill and Alex and Rocky had helped enormously after the burglary, too, so Mrs. Sunburg had been pleased to say yes when she'd been asked to watch Benjie for an hour after school today.

Mrs. Sunburg inhaled the sweet cinnamon-sugar smell of the cookie and decided it wouldn't hurt her diet too much if she ate one or two with Benjie.

While the cookies baked she washed the mixing bowl

and the measuring cups. Then she set out a glass for Benjie's milk and started a pot of coffee for herself.

He should be here any minute.

Rufus nudged her leg, an old sock in his teeth. The ends dangled downward on both sides of his mouth like a droopy mustache.

Mary had tied a knot in the sock, and it had become Rufus's favorite toy. He loved to bite the knot, shaking his head and growling furiously while someone tugged on the two ends of the sock.

"We're having company today," Mrs. Sunburg told Rufus. "Benjie will play with you when he gets here."

While the coffee brewed Mrs. Sunburg looked out the window, watching for Benjie to come running up the driveway. She smiled, remembering when her own two boys had been that age. They never walked; they only ran, hopped, jumped, or skipped.

A few minutes later, Mrs. Sunburg's smile was replaced by a worried frown. He really should have been here by now. Had he forgotten that he was supposed to come to her house?

Perhaps I should go next door, she thought. But the last pan of cookies still had six minutes to bake, and she didn't like to leave the house when the oven was turned on.

She dialed the Kendrills' number and got an answering machine. She did not leave a message.

She waited a couple of minutes and dialed again but hung up when the machine clicked on.

The oven timer rang. Mrs. Sunburg turned the oven off and put the cookies to cool with the others.

She stepped out to the front porch and listened for the sound of the departing school bus. She heard only the distant drone of a jet plane high overhead.

The Kendrills didn't seem like the kind of people who would make arrangements for her to watch their child and then not bother to call when she wasn't needed. The more she thought about it, the more uneasy she became.

Feeling both disappointed and apprehensive, she poured herself a cup of coffee and sampled a snickerdoodle. She would wait another five minutes. If Benjie still hadn't come, she would go over there and look for him.

Benjie knew that he couldn't let the bad guys see him. Mom and Dad and Alex had said the bad guys wouldn't kidnap anyone, but Benjie wasn't taking any chances. He decided to hide in the bushes until they left; then he would go in and call 911 before he ran to Mrs. Sunburg's house.

With his heart still pounding, Benjie jumped off the side of the porch. He dropped to his hands and knees and crawled behind the laurel bushes that lined the front of his house. He had to lie almost flat because the laurel bushes weren't very big yet. Mom had planted them last summer.

I should have gone to Mrs. Sunburg's house instead of coming home, Benjie thought. Mom told me I was supposed to go there today. She told me she wouldn't be home.

Benjie tried to hear what the burglars were saying or doing, but all he heard was a pair of crows cawing in the trees behind his house.

The damp dirt had a rich earthy smell. I'm wrecking my school clothes, Benjie thought. Mom's going to be mad when she sees mud on my good shirt.

Still the bad guys did not come out. Were they putting everything from the Kendrills' kitchen into boxes so they could steal it all?

Benjie hoped they didn't take the rooster cookie jar or Mom's china dishes. The set of dishes had belonged to Benjie's grandmother, and when she died, Benjie's mom had brought the dishes home and displayed them in a special cupboard that had glass doors. The pattern was called Buttercup and Mom always used them on Thanksgiving and Mother's Day.

If the bad guys took Mom's Buttercup dishes, Mom would be sad, and if they took the rooster cookie jar, Benjie would be sad.

Maybe I should run to Mrs. Sunburg's house now, Benjie thought, before the van leaves. If I call the police while the bad guys are still here, the police might catch them on their way out of Valley View Estates, and we'd get all of our things back.

He wished he had left his shoes on. He could run faster in them than he could in his socks.

Benjie slithered like a snake behind the bushes, keeping his head down and pulling himself forward with his arms until he reached the corner of the house that was closest to Mrs. Sunburg's house. The laurel branches scratched the back of his neck and snagged his shirt as he crept along. Small rocks and twigs dug into his forearms.

At the corner, he looked toward the trees and shrubs that divided the two homes. An area of grass stretched between Benjie's house and the trees. If he ran out there in the open, the bad guys might see him. Even if they stayed inside, they might look out the window.

What if they had guns?

Benjie shuddered. He would be an easy target, out in the grass.

Mom would be sad if she lost her Buttercup china, but Benjie knew she'd rather lose the dishes than lose him. People and animals are more important than things. He needed to save himself, and Lizzy, and Pete. He hoped Pete was in the house, hiding on top of the piano or under the table.

Instead of running to Mrs. Sunburg's house now, he decided to wait until the bad guys left. He would spy on them from the bushes and make sure they didn't steal Lizzy. He would memorize what they looked like so he could give a clear description of them to the police.

He wished he had his spy backpack with him, but even without it, he knew what to do. His best spy book told how to be a good witness, and Benjie had read it so many times, he knew it by heart.

He would stay hidden and look carefully at the men so that he could describe them accurately. Good spies notice details, and that's what Benjie intended to do. Good spies use their ears as well as their eyes. They even pay attention to smells. Benjie inhaled several times. He didn't smell anything except dirt.

Satisfied that he had made the right decision, Benjie crawled along the edge of the house toward the front door and waited for the men to come out.

He didn't have to wait long.

10

Benjie heard the bad guys come out of the house. Lying on his stomach, he peered cautiously between the laurel branches, trying to get a good look at the burglars without being seen himself.

Two men crossed the narrow porch toward the steps. The taller of the two wore a red-and-black plaid shirt. He closed the door of the house; Benjie heard it click. The other man's T-shirt protruded out over the top of his pants, which rode low on his hips. He had what Benjie's dad would call "a serious case of beer belly."

Details, Benjie told himself. Remember the details. They both wore faded jeans. The tall one had on a floppy brown hat; the chunky one had a stubbly beard. Both wore sturdy work boots that laced.

The bearded one carried a large cardboard box. Benjie couldn't see what was in it, but he could tell from the way the man moved that it was heavy.

"Be careful with those dishes," the tall one said. "They'll be worth more if they aren't chipped."

Mom's Buttercup, Benjie thought. Those mean men were stealing Mom's good dishes.

The men moved out of Benjie's line of sight, but he didn't dare shift position to keep watching them. He heard a van door shut and knew it was the rear door, where they had loaded everything in. He waited to give them time to get in themselves, but he didn't hear the other doors close.

As he thought about the van, he realized that he had forgotten the most important thing. He needed to get the number from the license plate. Then, as soon as the bad guys drove away, he could go inside and call the police and report what the van looked like and the license number, and the police would find it for sure.

I should have looked at the number right away while the bad guys were still in the kitchen, Benjie thought. Well, it wasn't too late. The van was still here.

Benjie eased his head from behind the bush, far enough so he could see the truck's license plate. 0 9 4 X C L.

Benjie found a twig and began scratching the numbers in the dirt under the laurel bush. If it was written down, he wouldn't forget it. 0 . . . 9 . . . 4 . . . As he worked, a dog barked somewhere in the next block. Benjie wished Rufus would come here and bark at the bad men and alert Mrs. Sunburg.

He formed the numbers carefully. He could hear the men talking as he worked, but he concentrated on his printing and didn't pay attention to what they said.

As he started to print the X, the twig snapped. Benjie held his breath, fearing the men had heard it and would come to investigate, but they didn't.

Pete finished the hamburger, tried one more time to open the glove compartment, and then jumped on the back of the seat. He needed to wash his whiskers, but he would do that after he got outside. He wished he had found something that would identify the crooks, but at least he'd had a good meal.

The back of the van was full now. The thieves had even taken the grandfather clock. Pete could no longer get to the floor or squeeze between the items. There were too many things crammed into the van, and Pete's stomach bulged from the hamburger and french fries.

He had to walk on top of the television set, then pick his way across the boxes. He was balanced on the handlebars of Alex's bike when he heard the men coming. Pete hunkered down, hoping they wouldn't notice him.

"You drive," one man said. "I never had a chance to eat my lunch, and I'm starving." He set one more box in the van.

The back door of the van slammed shut.

I should have left sooner, Pete thought. I could have car-

ried the hamburger in my teeth and eaten it outside the van. Now I'll have to jump past one of the men in order to get out.

Pete turned quickly and went toward the front again, planning to jump out when the man opened the door. I'll catapult past him, Pete thought. It's a good thing I've been practicing.

Before Pete could get into position, the door on the passenger's side opened.

"Hey!" the man said. "Somebody swiped my lunch."

"What are you talking about?" the second man said. "Who would want a cold hamburger?"

"Look at this! I left my burger and a box of french fries on the seat, and some lowlife got in here and ate them."

Pete crouched on top of Alex's bike, as close to the front as he could get without being seen. Both men now stood on the same side of the van, with the door open. Pete watched them over the top of the seat back, waiting for his chance to jump out without getting caught.

"Whoever it was made a mess," said the bearded man. "There's pieces of paper all over, as if he didn't bother to unwrap the burger before he bit into it."

"Maybe it was a dog."

"How would a dog get in here?" Using his fingers like a rake, the bearded man brushed the pieces of wrapper from his seat to the Kendrills' driveway. He leaned toward the floor and gathered the empty bag, the french-fry carton, the rest of the bits of wrapper, and all the candy wrappers and other trash that was there. He tossed it all outside. Let somebody else clean it up.

"It doesn't matter who did it," the tall man said. "What matters is that we need to get a move on. You can buy another lunch after we unload."

"I wanted this lunch," the bearded man grumbled. "I've been thinking about those french fries the whole time we loaded the van." He picked up more bits of wrapper and dropped them outside the van.

Through the windshield, Pete watched the tall man walk around the front of the van to the driver's side. When he saw the man's hand reach for the door handle, Pete jumped to the top of the seat back and got ready to catapult. He would launch himself at flying speed and be gone before the man could react.

The instant the door opened, Pete took off, shoving his hind legs hard into the seat and stretching his front paws forward. As Pete reached the opening, the man ducked down to sit in the van. Instead of flying past the man and landing on the driveway, as Pete had planned, he crashed into the man's shoulder.

"Yow!" Pete yelled as he fell back on to the seat.

"Hey!" said the tall man as he straightened up and rubbed his shoulder. He stood beside the van, put both hands on the seat, and leaned in toward Pete.

"Here's your culprit," he said to his partner. "A cat ate your lunch."

Pete hissed at the man, his ears flat, and his tail waving back and forth like a windshield wiper. Could he make it if he tried to jump again now? He didn't think so. The door was open, but the man's body blocked too much of the space.

Pete hopped to the floor between the two seats. He didn't like to turn his back on the first man, especially when the man was so close, but maybe he had a better chance of escaping out the other side.

As Pete looked that way, the bearded man got into the passenger's seat. At the same time the tall man sat behind the steering wheel. Pete was trapped in the space between the two seats.

The bearded man glared at Pete as he slammed the door shut. "I think I'll teach this cat a lesson," he said. "He ate every single one of my fries!"

"We aren't hanging around here while you take revenge on a stupid cat," the tall man said as he pulled his door closed.

"I'm not stupid," Pete said. "I'll match my IQ to yours, any day."

"I didn't mean now," the bearded man said. "I'll do it later."

Do what? Pete wondered. He didn't like these men, not one bit. He leaped onto the dashboard and stomped back and forth. "Open the door!" Pete yelled. "Let me out!"

"I'm not taking a cat with us," the tall man said. "Are you nuts? All we need is a cat howling and attracting attention. Listen to him: he sounds as if he's being tortured and you haven't laid a hand on him yet."

"That's right!" Pete cried. "I'll howl so loud the police will think someone's being murdered. You'll get pulled over. You'll get charged with kidnapping."

"Shut up, cat," the bearded man said, "or I'll give you a good reason to howl." He grabbed Pete by the scruff of the neck and hauled him onto his lap.

"You'll regret this," Pete said. "My claws are sharp, and my teeth are sharper."

The other man started the engine. "Put the cat outside," he said.

"No. I've decided to keep him."

"Suit yourself." The driver released the emergency brake and stepped on the accelerator. The van moved forward.

"Let me out!" Pete shrieked. He scrambled across the man's leg and pawed at the window. "Help! Let me out of here!"

Benjie finished scratching the last letter in the dirt. He heard the doors of the van slam shut.

The engine started.

Benjie dropped the twig and got ready to run. As soon as the van left, he would race inside, call 911, and tell the police about the bad guys. Then he'd go to Mrs. Sunburg's house. He listened carefully for the van to pull away, not wanting to waste a second.

When the van started to move, Benjie scrambled out of the bushes, climbed onto the porch, and yanked at the door. The knob didn't turn. The door was locked. He would have to go to Mrs. Sunburg's house to call 911.

As he turned away from the house, he heard a cat shrieking.

Pete! Pete was in trouble.

Horror brought goose bumps to Benjie's arms as he realized that Pete's cries came from inside the van.

The bad guys were stealing Pete!

Benjie ran down the porch steps and raced after the van, but it was already halfway down the long driveway.

Pete howled louder. When the bearded man picked him up and tried to shove him into the rear of the van on top of the bicycle, Pete bit him on the hand.

The man cursed and let go. Pete jumped to the back of the man's seat and clawed at the man's shoulder, ripping holes in his T-shirt and scratching his back. The man yelled and swatted at Pete.

The driver slammed on the brakes. "I can't drive when you're wrestling with a cat," he said. "I'll go off the road and hit a tree."

"The cat bit me!" the bearded man said. "He broke the skin. Look, I'm bleeding."

"And I'll bite you again if you don't let me out," Pete screamed.

"Then put him outside," the man in the plaid shirt said. "I told you we shouldn't take him with us."

"I'm not putting him out here. I'm going to throw him in the river when we go across the bridge." He turned, reached behind the seat, and grabbed Pete's tail.

Pete clung to the spokes of Alex's bicycle when the man tried to pull him by the tail to the front of the van. "Help!" he screeched. "Somebody help me!"

Benjie saw the brake lights go on. The van had stopped. He ran faster, gravel from the driveway kicking up behind his feet. He no longer cared if the bad guys saw him. He didn't care about calling 911. He didn't care about anything except getting Pete back.

He rushed to the door on the passenger's side of the van and tugged on the handle. It was locked. He could see Pete inside. The bad man was pulling Pete's tail.

Furious, Benjie pounded on the window with both fists.

11

S top that!" Benjie yelled.

Startled, the man let go of Pete's tail.

Pete crawled farther into the rear of the van, squeezing between the clock and the TV set until he reached the floor. The men couldn't reach him there without unloading everything.

Benjie banged on the window again. "Open this door!" he shouted. "You can't have Pete!"

The bearded man looked out the window at Benjie. "It's a kid," he said.

"Oh, great. Now he's seen us, and he can describe the van. I knew we should have gotten out of here sooner."

Benjie pounded harder. If they wouldn't open the door, maybe he could break the window. "Give me back my cat!" he yelled.

The bearded man rolled the window down a couple of inches. "What cat?" he said. "We don't have any cat."

"Yes, they do," Pete hollered. "I'm here, Benjie, in the back of the van."

"Well, what do you know," the tall man said, turning to look over his shoulder. "There IS a cat in the van." He opened his door and got out. "He must have sneaked in when we were parked at this house," he said.

"He didn't sneak in," Benjie said. "You stole him."

"We're a delivery service, kid. We were supposed to drop off a TV set, but nobody was home. We didn't know your cat got in the van."

Tears coursed down Benjie's cheeks, and his breath still came in gulps from running so fast. "You didn't try to deliver anything. You broke into our house and you're stealing Dad's clock and Alex's bike and Mom's good dishes, and you're trying to kidnap Pete and sell him for a lot of money, but you won't get away with it!"

The two men looked at each other. The driver held his door open wide. "Come on, cat," he said. "Get out of there." He raised his voice higher. "Here, kitty, kitty, kitty."

Pete wanted to jump out, but he was wedged so tightly between the TV and the clock he couldn't turn around.

"What makes you think we stole anything?" the bearded man said.

"Because I'm a spy and you're bad guys. I took down your license number and I know what you look like, and I'm going to call the police, and they'll catch you, and I hope they lock you up in jail for the rest of your lives!"

104

The bearded man got out of the van, too. "We don't want the cat," he said. "I tried to get him out, but he won't leave."

Benjie looked in the van. "Pete?" he said. "Where are you?"

"Go home, Benjie!" Pete said. "Call the sheriff!"

The tall man leaned toward his partner across the top of the van. "We've got a big problem," he whispered. "Only one way out, as I see it."

"We can't leave him here to spill the beans," the bearded man said.

"No. We can't."

The bearded man motioned for Benjie to get in. "The cat's hiding from us. He's on the floor, in back. You'll have to go in there and catch him."

"Don't do it, Benjie," Pete called. "I'm coming as fast as I can. I'll jump out."

"Here, Pete," Benjie said. "Don't be scared. I'll save you."

"That cat's wilder than a hoot owl," the tall man said. "You'll have to get in the van and coax him out."

Pete stood on his hind legs and hooked his front paws over one of the tires on Alex's bike. If he could pull himself up, he would be able to turn around and crawl to the front of the van. "I'm coming!" he yelled. "Don't get in the van!"

Benjie climbed into the van and knelt on the passenger's seat, facing the rear. He stretched his hands over the back of the seat toward Pete.

"I'll be okay," Pete told Benjie. "They'll let me go now. Don't wait for me. Run to Mrs. Sunburg's house, as fast as you can, and call the police."

"I see him!" Benjie said. He stood on the seat and leaned over the back, trying to reach Pete.

"Get out of the van!" Pete said. "I don't trust them. Run, Benjie! Run away from them!"

It was too late. As Benjie extended his hands toward Pete, the bearded man shoved him, knocking him sideways to the floor between the two seats.

As Benjie tried to scramble back onto the seat, the bearded man got in and closed the door. The man shoved him down. "Stay where you are," he said, "and don't make any noise."

Pete reached the top of the bike and jumped to the back of the driver's seat. The driver's door was wide open. Pete could easily have catapulted out and landed on the driveway by the tall man's feet, but he didn't do it. He couldn't jump to safety until Benjie was out of the van.

The tall man reached in and tried to grab Pete.

Pete hissed and slashed at the man's hand with his claws. "I'm staying with Benjie," he said. "He needs me to protect him."

The tall man drew his hand back. "This cat is a savage," he said. "He probably has rabies."

Pete jumped to the floor beside Benjie. He arched his back and puffed his fur out as far as he could. He gave his most *ferocious growl.* "Lay a hand on Benjie," *he roared,* "and you'll wish you hadn't."

Benjie reached for the door handle, with his other hand on Pete. "I have him now," he said. "He'll let me carry him out."

The bearded man opened his door. He reached down and tried to pick Pete up.

Pete bit the bearded man in the leg, but he got mostly a mouthful of the man's jeans. As his teeth sank into fabric, the tall man grabbed him from behind. The hand closed on the back of Pete's neck and yanked so hard that a clump of fur came out.

Pete clamped his teeth tight on the man's pants and dug in with his claws, but the jeans tore and Pete was lifted across the steering wheel toward the open door, with a piece of denim in his mouth and his four paws dangling helplessly downward.

"Get out, Benjie!" *he howled.* "Run!"

The tall man held Pete at arm's length for a second. Then he flung the cat as hard as he could throw. Pete landed in the gravel behind the van and lay still.

Benjie struggled to get up, to see what the tall man had done with Pete, but the bearded one put his hands on Benjie's shoulders and held the boy on the floor next to his boots.

"Don't move," he said.

The tall man slid behind the steering wheel, slammed

his door shut, and started the engine. The van careened out the end of the Kendrills' driveway and sped up Valley View Drive, with Benjie on the floor between the two burglars.

"Stay by my feet," the bearded man said as he held Benjie down with both hands. "Don't make any noise."

The will to fight drained out of Benjie as he realized he couldn't get away. He collapsed by the man's shoes like a piece of cooked spaghetti and lay there, crying quietly. Some spy he was. Not only had he failed to alert the police, he had let the bad guys trick him into getting in their van.

I never should have blurted out that I knew they were crooks, Benjie thought. If I hadn't done that, they might have given Pete to me and driven away. Then I could have called the police. A good spy keeps his mouth shut, but I blabbed everything I knew to the wrong people.

At least I saved Pete, Benjie thought. I did that one thing right.

From a hazy corner of his mind, Pete heard the van drive away. He lay in the gravel, too sore to get up. The fur was scraped off one ear where he had slid on it when he landed, and his head throbbed. He hoped he didn't have any broken bones.

Pete flexed one leg at a time. All four still moved. He slowly sat up, then licked one front paw and dabbed carefully at the scraped ear, washing off the blood.

He had to stop those men. He had to free Benjie. But

how? There was no use running after the van. He would never catch it.

He had to get help. He must let the people know where Benjie was.

Alex would be home soon, but Pete couldn't wait. Benjie needed help right away.

Pete had not yet met Mary's grandmother, but he knew that Benjie and Alex liked the older woman. If they liked her, Pete knew he would like her, too, and he was sure she would help.

He was too sore to run, but he walked as fast as he could toward Mrs. Sunburg's house. Maybe he could get her to follow him home, where she would notice that items were missing from the house.

Mrs. Sunburg finished her coffee, dialed the Kendrills' number again, and got the answering machine. This time she left a message.

"Benjie, are you there? It's Mrs. Sunburg. If you're home, pick up the phone." Nothing happened.

She put on a sweater and turned off the coffeemaker.

"I'll be back in a few minutes, Rufus," she said. "I'm going over to Benjie's house." Locking the door behind her, she left the house and started toward the Kendrills'.

She was partway there when a big white-and-brown cat trotted toward her, yowling loudly. The cat's eyes looked wildly from one place to the next, and his long dark tail thrashed like a whip. His left ear was bleeding, and he looked as if he had been rolling in the mud. Although the rest of his fur was thick, there was a bald spot the size of a half-dollar on the back of his neck.

"Gracious, kitty," Mrs. Sunburg said. "What happened to you?"

"They took Benjie!" Pete said. "They pushed him in the van and drove away!"

Pete hurried partway toward his own driveway, to show her where the van had been, then turned and went back to her. It still hurt to run, but Pete repeated the circle as quickly as he could, to convince Mrs. Sunburg how urgent the matter was. "Benjie needs help!" he cried as he trotted back and forth. "Those men took Benjie."

"Are you Alex's cat?" Mrs. Sunburg wondered. "Did Benjie go home and you got out and got in a catfight and now he's looking for you?"

"He isn't looking for me, but we need to look for him." Oh, it was so frustrating that the people couldn't understand anything Pete said. Pete had often wondered why the schools didn't offer classes in "Cat as a Second Language" so that humans would be able to converse as intelligently as the rest of the animal world does.

Mrs. Sunburg started toward the Kendrills' house again. "Benjie?" she called. "Are you here?"

"How could he be here?" Pete said. "I told you: two thugs took him away in a van."

Mrs. Sunburg reached the front of the house and saw a mess in the driveway. It looked as if someone had emptied their car's litter bag. How could people be so inconsiderate? Shaking her head, Mrs. Sunburg picked up an empty milk carton, candy wrappers, a cigarette package, and several pieces of paper.

"Don't do that," Pete said. "The burglars threw that trash there; it might be important evidence."

Mrs. Sunburg stuffed all the garbage into a discarded white paper bag from a fast-food restaurant. Then she knocked on the door. There was no answer. This is very strange, she thought. She tried to open the door, but it was locked. She walked around to the back door and knocked there. The house remained quiet.

The cat wasn't quiet, though. Clearly something had frightened the poor creature.

She knocked one last time, rapping loudly with her fist.

Pete stood beside her on his hind legs. With his front paws, he clawed at the door, hoping she would open it. If she went inside, she would see that burglars had been here, and she would call the police.

If Pete could get in the house, maybe he could find some clue that would help the people find Benjie.

It's going to be up to me, Pete thought. I'm the only one who knows what happened to Benjie. Since the humans can't understand what I tell them, I'll have to show them.

111

How could he show them? He wished he knew where to start.

When there was no response to her knock, Mrs. Sunburg tried the doorknob, but it didn't turn.

"I'm sorry, kitty," she said. "I know you want to go in, but the door is locked."

"Look in the window," Pete said.

Thoroughly worried now, Mrs. Sunburg headed back home. As she passed the Kendrills' garbage can, she lifted the lid and dropped the bag of litter inside.

"You're tampering with evidence," Pete said. "They won't find it there."

Mrs. Kendrill had left a phone number where she could be reached.

I should have come over sooner, Mrs. Sunburg thought.

Why was one of the cats outside? From the way he had tried to get into their house, she was certain this cat who kept yowling and running around her belonged to the Kendrills.

Feeling as if her thoughts were going in circles like the cat, Mrs. Sunburg found the number Mrs. Kendrill had given her.

"I need to speak to Anita Kendrill," she said.

"I'm sorry, she left a few minutes ago."

"Oh, no!"

"Is something wrong?"

"Do you know if she was going straight home?"

112

"I wouldn't know that. I can give you her home number, if you like."

"I already have it," Mrs. Sunburg said. "Thanks anyway." She hung up, then looked at the clock. Mary would be home in about ten minutes, which meant Alex would be home then, too. Mrs. Kendrill might be here even sooner. Once the Kendrills got home, they could look for Benjie inside. Had he let himself in, then fallen and hurt himself? If so, wouldn't he have called out when she knocked? Should she wait until Alex or his mother arrived to do anything more?

The cat now sat outside her back door, yowling mournfully. The cut on his ear didn't seem deep enough to cause such distress, and although he was dirty, he was able to move around. Something else was wrong.

She wondered if the cat might have been hit by a car and had some internal injury. She knelt beside him. Putting one hand on each side of Pete, she probed gently. He let her touch him without flinching, but he trembled as if he was in shock.

The cat's behavior convinced Mrs. Sunburg that he had seen something bad. But what?

If only animals could talk, Mrs. Sunburg thought. She would love to know what that cat was saying.

Mrs. Sunburg decided not to wait for Alex or his mother to get home. She picked up the phone and called the police.

12

I want to report a missing person," Mrs. Sunburg said. "A little boy."

"How long has he been gone?"

"He was supposed to come to my house after school, at three o'clock, and I was watching for him, but he never came."

"You aren't his mother, then?"

"No, I'm a neighbor."

"Have you contacted the boy's parents?"

"I tried to call his mother, but I can't reach her. I don't know where Benjie's father works, so I can't call him. You need to send an officer out here right away. Something bad has happened to Benjie, I know it. Even his cat is acting spooked."

"His cat?"

"Yes, the cat's not supposed to be outside, but he is, and Benjie's not here."

"I tell you what, ma'am," the officer said. "Why don't you wait until you've talked to one of the boy's parents, and then, if they don't know where the child is, they can call and give me more details."

"You already have the only detail you need," Mrs. Sunburg said. "Benjie is missing!"

"People often think a child is missing, but it almost always turns out to be a misunderstanding. Perhaps the boy went home from school with a friend. Maybe he missed the school bus, and he's waiting in the school office for someone to pick him up. Maybe he forgot that he was supposed to go to your house today, and he's off riding his bike somewhere. Maybe he was daydreaming or reading a book on the bus and didn't get off at his stop, and now he's walking home. Believe me, these things happen all the time."

"I'm sure they do," Mrs. Sunburg said.

"I suggest you call the boy's school, to see if he's still there. If he isn't, wait until you've talked with his parents before you panic. He's only forty-five minutes late; that isn't long enough to assume he's missing. I'm sure everything will be fine."

Mrs. Sunburg was not reassured. If Benjie had gone home with a friend or had missed his stop on the bus route or was sitting in the school office, who had let the cat out? Still she felt she had no choice but to do what the officer suggested.

She called the school next.

"This is Ruth Sunburg, Mary's grandmother," she told the secretary who answered. Then she explained about Benjie and asked if he was still at school.

"He isn't here in the office," the secretary said. "If you'll hold, I'll check with his teacher."

A few minutes later, the secretary came back on the line. "Benjie's teacher says he boarded the school bus, as always," she said. "She personally was the first-grade bus monitor today, and she knows that no student missed the bus."

"Do you have a phone number for Benjie's father?" Mrs. Sunburg asked. "His mother gave me a number, but when I called she had already left her meeting. I don't know how to reach Mr. Kendrill."

"I'm sorry. I'm not allowed to give out personal phone numbers."

"This is an emergency," Mrs. Sunburg said. "I don't know where Benjie is, and I'm afraid something has happened to him."

"Well . . ." The woman hesitated. "The rules about personal information were made clear when I took this job."

"I don't want to get you in trouble," Mrs. Sunburg said. "Perhaps I could speak to the principal."

"Hold on, please. I'll connect you."

When the principal answered, Mrs. Sunburg quickly explained the situation.

"I can't give you Mr. Kendrill's number," the principal said, "but I will call him immediately and ask him to call you."

"Thank you." Mrs. Sunburg hung up and waited for the phone to ring. She hoped the principal could reach Mr. Kendrill. Too much time was being wasted while she tried to notify someone that Benjie wasn't here. Although she agreed that private phone numbers should not be given out willy-nilly, she thought there were times when common sense was more important than rules, and this was one of those times.

She kept looking out the window, hoping to see Benjie, but all she saw was the brown-and-white cat. The cat was still yowling and running back and forth through the trees between the Kendrills' property and her own. Whatever that cat had seen, it had certainly upset him.

Pete's throat hurt from yelling so much, and it hadn't done one bit of good. I might as well save my breath, he thought. Mary's grandmother had paid attention to him only long enough to be sure he wasn't seriously hurt. No matter how many times he told her about Benjie, she never figured out what he was saying. If only people were as clever as cats.

Pete wished he had some water. Those french fries had been too salty.

Since he wasn't doing any good at Mary's house, he plodded back to his own house. His right front leg ached where he had landed on it when the man threw him out of the van. Pete favored the leg, causing him to limp.

He sniffed the front steps. He could tell where the burglars had walked. He sniffed some more around the spot where they had parked the van.

He followed the truck's smell halfway down the driveway, where he picked up the smell of the men again.

This is where they stopped, Pete knew. This is where the tall one caught me and threw me into the gravel. Pete's head and leg still throbbed where he had landed.

Benjie's scent was there, too. This is where Benjie had stood when he knocked on the window.

Pete's tail drooped down until the tip dragged in the gravel. I'm a failure as a spy cat, he thought. Instead of protecting Benjie, I sat in the van gobbling up cold hamburger. Now Benjie's life is in danger and I don't know how to help him.

Exhausted, Pete laid down in the grass beside the driveway and fell asleep.

Alex got off the school bus at Rocky's corner rather than riding all the way to his own stop. The boys talked awhile, making plans to get together as soon as they finished their homework.

Then Rocky went toward his house, and Alex walked home by himself.

"Alex!"

Alex saw Mary running toward him. She had ridden the bus home, too, but had gone on to her own stop when Alex got off with Rocky.

"Benjie didn't come to my house after school," Mary said. "He was supposed to go straight there when he got off the bus, but he never arrived."

Alex walked faster, and Mary fell into step beside him.

"Gramma tried to call your parents and can't reach either of them, and nobody answers the phone or the door at your house. She called the school, too, and Benjie's teacher said he got on the bus."

"He probably forgot that he was supposed to go to your house," Alex said. "Maybe he went home and got his spy backpack, and now he's in his secret spy place."

Pete woke up when Alex and Mary approached. He stood and hobbled toward them. "Benjie's been kidnapped," he called. "Two men took him away in a van!"

"Pete!" Alex said. "What are you doing outside?"

"He's limping," Mary said. "He's been hurt."

Alex picked Pete up and examined him. "His ear's cut," he told Mary, "and he's all dirty on one side. There's a bare spot on his neck, where the fur is missing."

"Never mind me," Pete said. "Benjie needs help."

Alex carried Pete around to the kitchen door. While Alex hurried to the garage and got the key that was hidden there, Mary knelt beside Pete and rubbed her fingers gently up and down his body, checking for unseen injuries.

Pete held still, enjoying the gentle massage.

Alex unlocked the door, stepped inside, and stopped, looking at the throw rug inside the door. "These are Benjie's school shoes," he said. "He came home."

"Thank goodness," Mary said.

"He's going to be in a heap of trouble when Mom and Dad find out he didn't go to your house when he was supposed to," Alex said. "Hey, Benjie! Where are you?"

Lizzy woke up, stretched, and came to rub against Pete.

"I think Pete's okay," Mary said, "although his one leg seems tender. Maybe I should ask Gramma to take a look at it."

"She already did," Pete said.

"That would be—" Alex stopped. "Oh, no!" he said, pointing to the cupboard with the glass doors. The doors stood open; the shelves were empty.

"What's wrong?"

"Mom's good dishes! They were in the cupboard and now they're gone."

"So is Benjie," Pete said.

Alex rushed to the family room. The computer desk was there, but the computer and printer were not. Neither was the TV.

"The burglars were here," Alex said. His legs felt weak, as if he had Rollerbladed too long. "They stole our VCR, and the computer, and the TV set."

"And Benjie."

"It was probably the same people who broke into my house," Mary said.

"That explains how Pete got out," Alex said. "They would leave the door open while they carried out our things." He gathered Pete into his arms and held him against his chest. "Is that how you got hurt?" he asked. "Did they kick you?"

"They threw me in the gravel," Pete said. "Hard."

"Don't touch anything," Mary said. "The sheriff will want to see the house exactly as we found it."

"Benjie!" Alex called. "Are you here?" When there was no answer, he set Pete down.

Alex and Mary rushed upstairs and looked in every room. What Alex saw made him feel sick to his stomach.

Dresser drawers had been turned upside down, their contents spilled on the beds. Sheets and towels had been flung out of the linen closet and lay in a heap on the hall-way floor.

"Benjie!" Alex called. "Benjie, where are you?"

"If he was here, he'd answer," Mary said. "Maybe he saw the burglars and got scared. Maybe he ran outside and hid somewhere."

"Without his shoes?"

"If he was frightened, he wouldn't take time to stop and put shoes on."

Alex picked up the phone in his parents' bedroom and dialed 911. "I want to report a burglary," he said, and gave the street address. "And my little brother's missing. He was supposed to go to our neighbor's house after school, but he never showed up, and he isn't at home, either, although I know he came here."

The emergency operator asked a few more questions, then said the sheriff was on his way.

"I need to let Gramma know what happened," Mary said. "She's already worried, and this is going to make her feel worse."

"I'm going to look in Benjie's hideout." Alex went down the stairs two at a time.

Alex ran out the kitchen door, with Mary behind him. She gave the door a shove, but it didn't close all the way.

"I'll ride my bike to the corner and back," Alex said as Mary started home. "It'll be faster." He stopped at the edge of the porch. He had left his bike there last night, but it wasn't there now. Mom must have put it in the garage before she left.

But when Alex went to the garage, his bike wasn't there, either. Anger bubbled inside him like water boiling in a pot. Alex had bought the bike with his own money, saved from his birthday, and from pulling weeds, and doing extra chores. Now those thieves had taken it.

Alex sprinted down the driveway, then ran down Elm Lane to the empty lot on the corner. "Benjie!" he yelled as he approached the clump of bushes where Benjie liked to hide. "Benjie!"

The spy hideout was empty.

13

*A*s soon as *Alex and Mary left, Pete went outside, too. He needed a nap, but he wasn't taking a chance of getting shut in the house.*

Lizzy started to follow him, but Pete hissed at her, to tell her to stay in. He would be busy showing the sheriff where the van had stopped; he couldn't be bothered watching after a kitten. Lizzy turned when he hissed, and ran under the table.

As Alex rushed back home he heard the rise and fall of sirens coming up the hill toward Valley View Estates. He waited at the end of his driveway until he saw the sheriff's car, then waved to let them know where to turn. The siren faded to a stop as the car headed down the driveway toward the Kendrills' house.

Sheriff Alvored and Deputy Flick got out of the car. Alex had met them at Mary's house, the night he saw the van. Mary and Mrs. Sunburg hurried toward them.

"Your dad called," Mary told Alex. "He's on his way home."

Rocky rode up on his bike. "I heard the sirens," he said. "What's happened?"

"The burglars broke into our house," Alex said, "and Benjie is missing."

"Missing?" Rocky said. "You mean, the burglars took Benjie?" Disbelief made his voice squeak.

Alex's throat was so tight with fear, he could barely answer. "We don't know if they took him," he said. "We only know he's gone."

Benjie's head hurt, and his nose was stuffed up from crying. He took a deep breath and forced himself to calm down. From where he was, hunched on the floor beside the bearded man's feet, he couldn't see out. He couldn't tell which direction the van was headed, but he knew it was going fast.

"A fine pickle you got us into," the driver of the van said.

"Me?" the other man said. "What did I do?"

"You insisted on keeping that cat. You should have tossed him out as soon as we found him. If the cat hadn't been howling, the kid wouldn't have run after us."

"How was I to know the boy would come home and hear the cat?"

"Not only does the boy see us, but he takes our license number and threatens to call the cops. If I hadn't been smart enough to lock the house when we left, he probably would have gone inside and called them. They could have caught us red-handed right there in the driveway."

"So what are we gonna do with him?" the bearded man said.

Benjie wiped his eyes with the back of his hand and listened. If the bad guys were going to talk about their plans for him, he needed to pay attention.

"You remember that old hunting cabin we went to last fall?"

"I remember."

"We're going there again."

"Forget it. That place was no good. I walked my legs off and never saw a deer."

"We aren't going to hunt for deer," the tall man said. "We're going to drop off the kid."

"We're taking him there? To that cabin?"

"As soon as we unload this stuff into the storage unit, we'll drive up there."

"That cabin's way up in the mountains. There's probably five feet of snow up there this time of year. How are we going to drive up that road?"

"We've got chains for the van."

"There's no heat in the cabin. There isn't even a woodstove."

"We won't be staying. Only the kid stays."

"You mean, leave him there? He'll freeze."

"That's the point."

There was a brief silence before the bearded man said, "I'm not so sure that's a good idea, Vance."

"Do you have a better plan?"

"No, but—"

"I didn't think so."

"Hey, man. You're talking about murder. If the cops caught us, we'd never get out of prison."

"The cops won't catch us. Use your head, Porker. It'll be spring or summer before the body is found, and there'll be no way to connect us to it."

"I don't like this."

"I don't like it, either, but unless you want to go to jail for all those burglaries, we have to be sure this kid never talks."

"I guess you're right."

"I'm always right."

The van hit a pothole. Benjie bounced, knocking his knees on the floor. Tears stung his eyes again, but he remained quiet, thinking about what the men had said.

He couldn't let them drive him to a wilderness cabin and leave him. He would have to escape.

Benjie made a plan. Good spies always have a plan. When the men stopped at the storage unit, he would see if other people were nearby. If he saw anyone, he would holler and honk the horn and create a huge ruckus. Whoever heard him would know something was wrong.

But what if there were no other people at the storage

unit? Then he would have to run while the men were unloading the van. They'd be distracted by their work, so he might get enough of a head start that they wouldn't be able to catch him.

I'll pretend to be asleep, Benjie thought. If they think I'm sleeping, they might leave me alone in the front of the van while they unload everything out the back.

While the bad guys were busy carrying things into the storage unit, Benjie would jump out and run away from them. He could hide somewhere, or flag down a passing car, or run to the storage company's office and call for help.

I know their names now, he told himself. Porker and Vance. I know what the van looks like, and when I call home, I can tell Mom or Dad to look in the bushes where I wrote down the license number. Maybe I'm not such a bad spy, after all.

"I need food," the bearded one, Porker, said. "I can't unload all this until I have something to eat."

"How can you think of your stomach now?" Vance said. "Don't you understand we're in big-time trouble? The kid's mother has probably already called the cops."

"So what? They don't know who to look for. The boy is the only one who saw us, and he can't tell anybody."

"We think he's the only one who saw us. We hope he is. But we don't know that for sure. We aren't wasting time buying food. You can eat after we get back from the cabin."

"It takes almost two hours to drive up there. I'll faint from hunger by then. If you get stuck in the snow, I'll be too weak to push the van. Come on, Vance. It'll only take five minutes to buy a hamburger and french fries. We can use the drive-up window."

Do it, Benjie thought. Stop as many times as you want.

It was already getting dark outside, so Benjie knew it must be close to 4:30. Vance was right; Mom would have called the police by now. Maybe someone else did see the van. Mrs. Sunburg might have come to look for Benjie as the van drove off, or someone else might have noticed the van drive away. Maybe the police already had a description.

"There's too much chance that the kid would attract attention if we stop," Vance said. "He could yell for help when they hand the bag of food through the window."

"I'll keep him quiet."

Benjie cringed at the man's tone of voice.

"We aren't stopping anywhere except the storage unit."

The two men rode on in silence.

Benjie hoped that the police were searching for him, but he knew he couldn't count on them finding him in time. He had to try to save himself.

He put his head on the floor, closed his eyes, and pretended to be asleep. Determined to make his escape, Benjie huddled on the floor and waited.

14

Benjie heard the van engine go slower. He leaned sideways to keep his balance as the van turned, but he still pretended to be asleep.

He could tell the tires were on gravel now, rather than a paved road. The men must be almost at their destination.

Benjie listened, trying to hear any noises outside the van.

"Good," Vance said. "There's no one else here. We have the place to ourselves. We can unload everything and get out of here before we're seen."

Disappointment made Benjie's throat tight. It wouldn't do any good to yell for help if there was no one near enough to hear him. He would have to run away.

A few seconds later the van stopped, then backed up, as if into a parking space.

Benjie kept his eyes closed, not moving. He took long, deep breaths, letting the air out through his mouth so that it made a faint hissing sound. He sensed that the men were looking at him.

"He's asleep," Porker whispered. "Let's leave him here while we unload."

Vance didn't answer, but he must have nodded agreement, because Benjie heard both side doors open. The men got out, then quietly pressed the doors closed behind them so as not to wake Benjie.

Benjie didn't move.

The rear door opened, and at the same time Benjie heard a sound like an overhead garage door rolling up. He knew that must be the entrance to the storage unit. The two men began lifting something out of the back of the van. Probably Alex's bike, Benjie thought, since it had been on top.

It was hard for Benjie to time his move when he couldn't see what the men were doing. Since his only hope of escaping was to get a good head start, he had to run when the men had their backs turned; otherwise they'd catch him for sure.

He opened his eyes a slit, just enough to squint through. Keeping his head on the floor, he slid forward until he could see between the two seats. One man was rolling Alex's bike into the storage unit. The other was carrying a box.

They left those items and came back for more boxes.

While Benjie waited he decided he should leave something in the van that would identify him. If Alex or his parents found the license number, the police might stop the van, but with Benjie gone and all the stolen goods unloaded, there would be nothing to prove that the burglars had used this van.

He wished he had worn his Mariners cap. An article of clothing would be the perfect evidence, but he couldn't leave his shirt or his pants.

Benjie reached his hand down and slipped the sock off his right foot. He wadded it into a ball, opened the glove compartment, shoved the sock inside, and closed the compartment.

Benjie decided he would run when they took out the grandfather clock. That was the most breakable item and an expensive one. It would take both men to carry it, and he thought they would pay careful attention while they hauled it from the van to the storage area.

He peeked at the men. They were hauling the TV set to the storage unit now and had turned a light on inside. The storage unit was the size of a single-car garage, and it was packed with boxes and electronic items. He saw several computers, television sets stacked three deep, and boxes piled on a wooden desk. He wondered if some of the goods belonged to Rocky's family, and to Mary and Mrs. Sunburg.

You creeps, Benjie thought as the men set the Kendrills'

TV on the floor. I'm going to escape and call the police and you'll be sorry you took all this.

He put his head down again and listened as the men returned to the van.

When they started to slide the clock out, Benjie looked through the slits in his eyes again. Nervousness made his breath come faster. It was almost time to make his move.

"Be careful," Vance warned. "This clock should be worth a bundle."

Benjie watched. It was dark out now, but the light from the storage unit spilled toward the van. The men kept the long clock flat on its back while each of them grasped one end. Vance had the end closest to the storage unit. He carried the clock with his arms behind him so that he could walk forward and see where he was going.

When they stepped away from the van with the clock between them, Benjie shoved open the door beside him and rolled out of the van, keeping his head down so he wouldn't be seen.

A light came on inside the van as the door opened. Benjie hadn't thought about that. Quickly he pushed the door closed until the light went off, holding his breath for fear one of the men would notice, but they both had their backs to the van.

"Walk faster," Vance said.

"I'm going as fast as I can. This thing is heavy."

"Well, don't drop it. Set it down gently."

Benjie bolted. His feet skimmed the surface of the gravel, barely touching down before he lifted them again. His arms pumped, and he stretched his legs out as far as he could with each step, willing himself to go faster.

As he ran he looked around, hoping to see someone who could help him. There were no people, and no other vehicles, only rows of storage units stretching ahead on both sides.

Benjie wasn't sure if he was running toward the street or toward the back of the storage lot. He didn't hear any traffic sounds. He came to the end of a row of storage units and turned the corner, looking for some place to hide.

The whole storage area was dimly lit with occasional streetlights, but he saw no shrubs or other hiding place, only the flat gravel road and another long row of storage units, their dark doors closed. Each one looked exactly like all the others except for the numbers over the doors.

The sharp bits of gravel cut into the bottom of his bare foot. Maybe it hadn't been such a good idea to leave his sock in the van. He was pretty sure his foot was bleeding.

The gravel soon wore a hole in his remaining sock, and he got a stitch in his side. His breath came in gasps, but he didn't slow down.

From the row he had left behind came a shout: "Hey! Vance! He's gone!"

They knew.

15

Benjie knew the men would hunt for him now. They would drive the van past every row of storage units until they spotted him.

Panicked, he looked for someplace, anyplace, to hide. He ran to the nearest unit and pulled on the door handle, hoping the door might be unlocked, but it didn't budge. He ran to the next unit; that one was locked, too.

He heard the van doors slam.

The van engine started, died, started again.

Go the other way, Benjie pleaded silently. Please! Don't come this way!

He came to the end of a row and looked in both directions. To his right, he saw only the road and more storage units, but to his left he saw a large dark shape, up close to one of the units. A big box? A piece of furniture? Benjie turned that way and ran toward the object. Whatever it was, perhaps he could hide behind it or underneath it.

As he drew closer, he saw that someone had left a clothes

washer and dryer outside one of the storage units. The washer and dryer were shoved up tight against the roll-up door, side by side, as if their owner had brought too much furniture to store and couldn't make the washer and dryer fit inside.

Benjie put his hands on the flat sides of the washer and tugged, trying to pull it away from the building far enough for him to squeeze in behind it. If he was in back of the washer, the bad guys might not see him when they drove past.

But the washer was too heavy. He couldn't slide it on the rough gravel, and it weighed too much for him to lift. He couldn't move the dryer, either.

I'll have to crouch beside the washer or dryer, Benjie thought. The men won't see me if they come from the other direction.

But what if they didn't? What if they came from the side he was on? The headlights would pick up Benjie's striped shirt and dark jeans against the white appliance, and he would be trapped.

Benjie hesitated. Which way would the men come? He had a fifty-fifty chance of choosing the right side. He decided those odds weren't good enough, not when his life was at stake.

Benjie yanked open the dryer door and stuck his head inside. He would fit.

He put one leg in, then sat in the dryer while he lifted

the other leg in. He had to sit doubled over, with his knees drawn up under his chin.

Leaning out, he grabbed the bottom of the door and pulled it almost all the way closed. He didn't shut it completely because there wasn't any handle on the inside and he feared he wouldn't be able to get it open again. It wouldn't do him any good to save himself from the bad guys only to suffocate in a clothes dryer.

He felt like a pretzel, with his arms crossed under his knees and his shoulders hunched over.

Instead of being smooth, like the outside of the appliances, the dryer drum had ridges every foot. When Benjie tried to lean back to get more comfortable, one of the ridges pressed into his backbone.

It was black as midnight inside the dryer, and Benjie felt too confined. He had heard that some people get panicky in elevators or other small spaces, and he could see why.

Seconds after he got inside the dryer, he heard the van approaching. For a brief moment its headlights lit up the small crack where the dryer door was open.

Benjie held his breath. Keep going, he thought. Don't stop.

He heard the van pass. The crack of light dimmed and was dark again. He heard the crunch of the tires moving away.

Benjie let his breath out.

He waited, in case the van went by again. He didn't

know how many rows of storage units there were in this complex, but he was sure the bad guys would drive past all of them, looking for him.

They knew he was on foot. They knew he couldn't have gone too far. They might drive past all of the storage units more than once before they gave up and left without him. It would be a mistake to get out of the dryer too soon no matter how uncomfortable he was.

Good spies are patient.

Benjie sat as still as if he were a load of laundry forgotten in the dryer. He didn't like being in there, but it was the only hiding place he had. A good spy does whatever is necessary to save a life, especially his own.

He decided he would count to five hundred before he climbed out of the dryer. By then, surely the men would be gone.

One, two, three . . .

Benjie began the long count.

Gravel spun out from behind the van's rear tires as Vance went around the corner from one row of storage units to the next.

"Where IS he?" he asked. "We were only parked there for ten minutes. How far can a little kid get on foot in ten minutes?"

Porker didn't answer. He didn't know where the kid was, and he didn't know how far a boy could run in ten minutes.

He knew only that his shoulder hurt where the cat had scratched him, his hand hurt where the cat had bit him, he had hunger pains, and now Vance was worked into a snit. Nothing about this day had turned out the way they had planned.

"Let's go," Porker said. "Leave him here."

"We can't. He said he got the license number."

"No little kid is going to remember a license number, especially when he's scared out of his wits."

"He wasn't too scared to get away from us. Even if he forgets the number, he can describe the van. He can identify us."

"Come on, Vance. Let's leave. If you're so worried about the van, we'll ditch it. We'll wipe it down so there aren't any of our fingerprints inside, and we'll report it as stolen. We'll say it's been missing a couple of hours. That'll give us an alibi in case the kid does remember the license number."

"Sometimes you surprise me," Vance said. "That isn't a bad idea. We'll get rid of the van and hot-wire a car to drive home in, and nobody will be able to connect us with the burglaries."

"Good. So let's get out of here. I'm starving."

Vance made a U-turn and went back the way they had come.

"What are you doing? The exit is the other direction."

"Did you see that washer and dryer that somebody left outside their unit?"

"What about them?"

"They looked almost new. No point in leaving a brand-new washer and dryer outside, asking to be stolen."

Porker groaned. "I'm tired, Vance. And I thought you were in a hurry to get rid of the van."

"It'll only take us a couple of minutes to put those appliances in our own unit." Vance saw the washer and dryer in the headlights again. He approached them slowly this time so he could get a better look. He pulled up beside the two appliances and stopped with the rear door of the van next to the washer.

"We'll get three hundred dollars for this set," he said. "Not a bad profit for five minutes of work."

"I've worked enough today. My back hurts, and I'm hungry."

"Can't you think of anything but food?"

"Can't you think of anything but money?"

"Three hundred bucks will buy a lot of french fries. Besides, you owe me one for trying to keep that wild cat and getting us stuck with the kid in the first place."

"Oh, all right." Porker opened his door and stepped out. "It'll be faster to take them than to talk some sense into you."

Vance got out, too. Their shoes made a crunching sound on the gravel as they walked toward the washer and dryer.

16

Pete crouched on the porch steps while his tail swept wildly from side to side. He tried to hold it still, but when he was nervous his tail had a mind of its own, completely out of Pete's control.

Sirens and flashing lights and strangers talking were enough to make most cats run for their lives, but Pete stayed where he was. He was the only one who knew what had happened to Benjie. If he was going to help Benjie now, he needed every scrap of information he could get.

He had given up trying to tell the people about Benjie and the van and the two men. Every time he spoke, they thought he wanted food. As if he could eat at a time like this!

Pete listened as Alex told the sheriff and his deputy what had happened. Mrs. Sunburg told her part of the story, too, and before she had finished, Mrs. Kendrill drove up.

"What happened?" she asked.

Everyone spoke at once, telling her about Benjie and about the burglary.

"He's still missing?" The color drained out of Mrs. Kendrill's face, and she leaned against her car as if she might topple over without support.

Sheriff Alvored made a call on his cell phone, reporting that Benjie was missing. Soon a second sheriff's car pulled up behind the first one; Deputy Harper and Deputy Ebbin got out. Then Mr. Kendrill arrived, and the stories got told all over again.

Mrs. Sunburg explained how nobody had answered the door when she came over to look for Benjie. "The cat was hurt, too," she said. "When I called the police, I should have told them that Benjie lived in an area that's been burglarized recently. Perhaps they would have come more quickly." She twisted the bottom of her sweater as she talked.

"It isn't your fault, Gramma," Mary said. "You did what you could."

"Do you have a recent picture of Benjie?" one of the deputies asked. "One that we can take to give to the media?"

"We have his new school picture," Mrs. Kendrill said. "He brought the packet home on Friday, and I stuck the large one on the fridge. Come on in."

"Mary and I will go home," Mrs. Sunburg said as the others headed for the house. "Call if we can help."

Rocky hesitated but stayed were he was.

Alex could tell that Mary wanted to stay, too, but her grandma took her by the arm. "We don't want to be in the way," she said. "We've told them everything we know."

When the people started toward the front door, Pete jumped off the porch into the shrubbery, intending to wait until the last person went inside before he followed. There was less chance of getting accidentally stepped on if he went in last.

He landed in the dirt beside one of the laurel bushes—and saw what looked like a word scratched in the dirt. Pete went closer, his nose to the ground. His whiskers twitched as he inhaled deeply.

Benjie had been here. His scent was everywhere in these bushes, and a twig that lay in the dirt next to the word smelled strongly of Benjie, too.

Pete crept to where he could see the word right side up, being careful not to step on any of the writing. He stood beside it, but it wasn't a word he recognized. He tried to sound it out in his mind and realized it wasn't a regular word at all. Words are made of letters; this was both letters and numbers.

0 9 4 X C L. Pete concentrated, trying to think where he had seen numbers and letters strung together like that.

It's a license-plate number, Pete realized. The cars and trucks all have a combination of letters and numbers on their license plates.

Benjie must have seen the burglars and decided to spy on

them. He hid from them here in the bushes, and he scratched this license number in the dirt using the twig for a pencil.

Pete knew this was important evidence. He needed to show it to the humans. "Look what I found!" he yelled. He leaped back up on the porch steps and saw that he had waited too long. The front door was closed. All the people had gone inside.

Pete pawed at the door. "Come out!" he called. "I found something that will help."

Alex opened the door. "Good boy," he said. "You came home."

Pete did not go inside. He jumped off the porch and landed beside the laurel bush. "Come here," he told Alex. "Look what I found."

"Get in here, Pete," Alex said. "This is no time to play games. Benjie's missing."

"I know all about it," Pete said. "I saw it happen, and now I found what Benjie scratched in the dirt. Come down here and look."

"Do you want me to try to catch him?" Rocky asked.

"No. He'd run from you." Alex closed the door.

Pete walked along the edge of the house to the corner, following Benjie's scent, but found nothing else of importance.

He went back to the front of the house and sat on the bottom step, waiting for the people to come out. It seemed to take much too long. What are they doing in there? Pete wondered.

This calls for drastic action, Pete decided. He had to make one of the people look at what he'd found. He threw back his head and shrieked his most bloodcurdling yowl, the one that made it sound as if he were being attacked by a mountain lion.

Alex flung open the door and rushed out, followed by Rocky. They stopped when they saw Pete on the step. "What's the matter with you?" Alex said. "Get inside."

Pete backed out of Alex's reach.

"Is he hurt?" Rocky asked. "My mom's home. She could drive him to the vet."

"I'm not going to the vet." Pete went into the bushes again. "Look what I found," he said.

"If he won't come in," Alex said, "I'm not chasing him." He slammed the door shut.

Pete forgave Alex for being cranky. He knew Alex was worried about Benjie. People, like cats, are not at their best when they're upset, and they sometimes say things they regret later.

Pete sat down on the step and washed his sore ear while he waited.

At last the door opened, and Sheriff Alvored came out. He stood in the open doorway talking to Mr. and Mrs. Kendrill, who were behind him.

Sheriff Alvored had a colored photo of Benjie in one hand. He held it up, turning it to the light so that he got a better view.

"It's good to have such a recent picture," he said. "I've had cases where the only photo the parents had of their child was two or three years old. Kids change a lot in two or three years. This will help a lot."

Pete looked at the sheriff, and at the photo. He could think of only one way to make the people follow him into the bushes so they would find the writing in the dirt.

Pete took a deep breath and clenched his teeth, knowing it would hurt his sore leg to push off hard enough to jump as high as he needed to go. It's a good thing he had practiced catapulting every day.

He stared at the sheriff's hand, taking aim.

As the sheriff examined Benjie's picture, Pete soared upward.

Mrs. Kendrill screamed.

Thud! Pete hit the sheriff's chest, right above his badge. The sheriff automatically raised the hand that held the photo, to protect himself, while the other hand went for the gun in his holster. As Pete dropped backward, he snatched the picture in his teeth.

Pete landed on his side, sending a sharp pain through his shoulder, but he couldn't stop yet. He rolled off the edge of the porch toward the laurel bush, still holding the picture of Benjie in his teeth. He carried it under the bush, where the people couldn't reach it without coming close to the writing.

All the people talked at once.

"What was that?" said Deputy Flick as he stepped out-side and aimed his gun into the bushes toward Pete.

"Don't shoot!" said Alex. "It's my cat!"

"What is he, an attack cat?" asked Deputy Flick.

"He took the picture of Benjie," Sheriff Alvored said, shaking his head as if he didn't quite believe what had just happened. "Grabbed it right out of my hand before I could react."

"Pete's gone crazy," Mr. Kendrill said. "Why would he take Benjie's picture?"

"He's never done anything like that before," Mrs. Kendrill told Sheriff Alvored. "Are you all right?"

"I'm fine. He startled me, that's all, flying at me out of the blue like that. I saw him sitting there, but I thought he was a pet cat."

"He is," Alex said. "But he's acted crazy ever since I got home. He's scratched and limping and there's a tuft of fur missing on his neck. Something happened to him this afternoon."

"Come here!" yelled Pete. "Come in the bushes."

"Alex," Mrs. Kendrill said, "get that picture away from Pete. Then bring him inside and lock him in the bathroom. We have enough trouble right now without him causing more."

"You sure that isn't some kind of wild cat?" Deputy Flick said. "Listen to him. It's enough to wake the dead."

"He's scared," Alex said.

Alex and Rocky walked past the sheriff and his deputy, who were putting their guns away, and stepped off the porch into the bushes near Pete.

Pete dropped the picture of Benjie right beside the place where Benjie had scratched numbers and letters in the dirt. He stood beside the photo, ready to grab it again if Alex didn't notice the writing.

"This isn't funny, Pete," Alex muttered. "The sheriff needs that picture." He put his hand down to pick the picture up, but he was looking at Pete, not at the ground.

Pete put both front paws on the picture and stood still. Now Alex couldn't pick up the picture without first picking up Pete, and he would have to lean down more in order to do that.

Alex bent over, stretched both hands toward Pete, and stopped. He looked at the dirt next to the photo.

"Do you see it?" Pete said. "I think Benjie wrote it. He was here. His scent is in the bushes."

"Did you get it?" Mrs. Kendrill said. "If not, I'll get the smaller photos."

Alex turned to Rocky. "Look at this," he said.

Rocky squatted beside Pete. "It looks like a license number," he said.

"That's what I thought," Alex said. He picked up the picture, then beckoned to the sheriff. "You need to look at this," he said. "Someone has written what seems to be a license number in the dirt under this bush."

Sheriff Alvored stood beside Alex while Rocky held back the laurel branches so the sheriff could get a better look.

"This hasn't been here long," Sheriff Alvored said. "It's right next to the downspout, so it would not be this distinct after water flowed across it. We had a hard rain this morning; this was written after that."

"Do you suppose Benjie hid in the bushes and spied on the burglars?" Rocky said.

"It's exactly the kind of thing he would do," Alex said. "One of his books even suggests writing a license number in the dirt if you don't have pencil and paper available. I remember reading that part to him."

"Yes," Pete said. "Now you're catching on."

"He isn't going to attack me again, is he?" asked Sheriff Alvored.

"No," Alex said. "I think he took the picture as a way to make us look under the bush."

The sheriff raised his eyebrows as he looked at Alex, then at Pete, then back to Alex.

"Take this down," he said to the deputy. "Zero, nine, four, X, C, L."

Deputy Flick wrote the numbers and letters down. Then Deputy Flick spoke into his phone. "We're issuing an all-points bulletin for this license number." He repeated the number twice. "The occupants may have a hostage, a seven-year-old boy. Use extreme care."

Alex handed the photo of Benjie to the sheriff, who gave it to Deputy Harper.

"We'll scan it and send it out right now," Deputy Harper said. She and her partner headed to their car. "Then we'll cruise the area."

Mr. Kendrill said, "You have a computer in the patrol car?"

"Deputy Harper is a computer genius," Deputy Flick said. "Her car is a portable office."

"Looks to me as if this was written with a twig," Sheriff Alvored said. He got a camera from the patrol car, took some pictures of the writing in the dirt, then carefully put the twig in a plastic evidence bag.

While the people all crowded around to see the writing in the dirt and speculated about whether or not Benjie had written it, Pete crawled out from under the laurel bush, limped up the porch steps, and went slowly into the house. He had done all that he could to help Benjie. Now it was up to the humans.

Pete ached all over, his ear still hurt, and he was too tired even to eat. He went straight to his bed, flopped down, and closed his eyes. Being a spy was hard work.

17

"What can I do to help?" Rocky asked as soon as the sheriff and all the deputies left.

"Let's make a flyer about Benjie," Alex suggested. "We can put copies on light poles and street-sign posts."

"Yes, flyers might help," Mrs. Kendrill said. "Say that he was wearing jeans, his red-and-white-striped polo shirt, and no shoes." Her voice shook as she described Benjie's clothes.

Mr. Kendrill took a large white envelope from the desk. Inside were Benjie's school pictures. He handed the five-by-seven picture to Alex.

"Put his picture on the flyer," he said, "and have color copies made." He gave Alex some money for the copies.

"Mom will drive us to town to make copies," Rocky said. "We can put them on all the telephone poles and at the school and in front of the post office."

"You can post flyers at the school and post office

tonight," Mrs. Kendrill said, "but save the rest. I don't want you boys going all over town after dark."

"You can put the rest up first thing tomorrow morning if we don't have Benjie back by then," Mr. Kendrill said.

Alex nodded. What if Benjie wasn't found tonight?

"I think we should drive around the area and look for him," Mrs. Kendrill said.

Mr. Kendrill agreed. "We don't know for sure that he is with the burglars. He may have been frightened and decided to hide somewhere, and now he doesn't realize it's safe to come home."

Alex didn't see how Benjie could have missed hearing all the sirens in the last hour. If Benjie was hiding in the neighborhood, he would know the sheriff had come and that it was safe to return home.

Alex didn't say that, though. He sensed that his parents would feel better if they did something specific, such as driving around looking for Benjie, rather than waiting passively for the phone to ring.

"Sheriff Alvored's card with his cell-phone number is next to the kitchen phone," Mr. Kendrill said. "We'll have our cell phone on in the car."

As Alex watched his parents drive away, he felt Rocky's hand on his shoulder.

"Do you have some colored markers?" Rocky asked.

Alex got the markers, and the boys set to work on the flyer. When it was done, Rocky called his mom. She drove them to the copy center and then to the school and post office.

"I'm scared for Benjie," Alex told Rocky as they tacked a flyer to the community bulletin board outside the post office. "I'm afraid the burglars caught him spying on them and got angry."

"He's a smart kid," Rocky said. "If he's been kidnapped, maybe he'll figure out a way to escape."

"I wish I could do more to help find him," Alex said.

"When we get back to your house, let's walk around outside and look for more clues."

As the car backed out of the parking spot at the post office, the headlights shone on Benjie's smiling face and the word MISSING.

Alex felt as if he were watching a horror movie or having a nightmare. What if Benjie was never found?

Alex's parents were still gone when the boys got home. Rocky's mom invited Alex to have dinner at their house, but the boys wanted to wait at Alex's house, in case there was any news of Benjie.

The boys got flashlights and walked all around the outside of the house but found no other clues. Then Alex made popcorn. Rocky filled a bowl and sat at the table, but Alex sat on the floor beside Pete's bed.

"Pete saw the writing in the dirt," he said as he petted the cat. "He stole the picture and took it under the bush so we'd go there and find the writing."

Pete purred as Alex stroked his side.

"I wonder what else he knows," Rocky said.

"Plenty."

Alex looked closely at Pete's cut ear and the bare spot on his neck. "How did you get so scraped up? Did you fight with another cat?"

I fought with the burglars. I tried to save Benjie from getting kidnapped.

Lizzy came out from under the couch and rubbed against Alex's leg. "Mrowr?" she said.

"Okay, you guys, quit begging," Alex said. "I'll feed you."

Lizzy scampered after Alex into the kitchen, but Pete stayed where he was. There had never before in Pete's life been a time when he didn't rush toward the sound of the can opener, but he didn't feel like eating now. Not when Benjie was gone.

"Come on, Pete," Alex called. "You deserve kitty num-num tonight."

Kitty num-num? Pete's all-time favorite treat? Pete's nose twitched as the delicious smell of whitefish and tuna drifted toward him. He got to his feet. Perhaps he could eat a small amount, after all.

As Pete ate, he saw Alex drop the empty num-num can into the wastebasket under the sink. Then Alex picked up the full wastebasket and headed for the kitchen door.

Pete remembered the rubbish that the burglar had tossed out of the van and Mrs. Sunburg had picked up. Here's my chance, Pete thought.

When Alex opened the kitchen door Pete dashed out, but instead of running off as he usually did, he stayed beside Alex.

Alex lifted the lid of the garbage can. Before he could empty the wastebasket, Pete jumped into the half-full garbage can and picked up the white paper bag in his teeth.

"Now what?" Alex said. He took the bag from Pete and shook out the contents. "Rocky!" Alex called.

Rocky rushed outside.

Pete jumped down.

"This bag of trash was in our garbage can," Alex said. "There are candy wrappers from licorice candy, but no one in my family likes licorice." He picked up an empty cigarette pack. "Nobody smokes, either."

He reached for two crumpled pieces of paper that had been in the bag and opened them. "This is our phone number," he said, handing one of the papers to Rocky. "The other paper has a street address on it. Who put this in our garbage can?"

"I don't think burglars would bother to throw their trash in the garbage can," Rocky said. "Could it have been one of the deputies?"

The boys thought back to when the sheriff and the deputies had been there. "None of them carried a bag like this," Alex said.

"The sheriff said to report anything unusual," Rocky said. "I think we should call him."

"Yes," Pete said. "Call the sheriff."

Alex dialed Sheriff Alvored's cell-phone number.

Pete ate his num-num and went back to bed.

Sheriff Alvored and Deputy Flick sat in their patrol car, drinking cups of coffee. The two men had been partners for more than ten years, and they often brainstormed ideas about what a criminal's next move might be. More than once their hunches had paid off with an arrest.

Their method was simple: think like a criminal. Try to figure out what the criminal might do next.

"This is the fourth burglary in three days in this area," Sheriff Alvored said. "All of them followed the same pattern, so it's likely the same burglars. What I'm wondering is, how are they getting rid of so much stolen property, so fast? Where are they taking it?"

"They can't be selling it as quickly as they steal it," Deputy Flick agreed. "The flea markets are only open weekends, and there hasn't been time for the thieves to run ads in *The Little Nickel* or some other paper. Maybe they're taking it to pawnshops."

"Maybe. But some of these items are awfully big and distinctive for the pawnshops. Where are they going to get rid of a grandfather clock?"

"What's your guess?" Deputy Flick asked.

"Jim's Second Hand Store? He buys from anybody that walks in the door, and the place is big enough to handle large quantities."

"I checked there this morning on my way to work. Jim has a new sign, 'I Buy Junk and Sell Antiques,' but I looked through the whole store, and he didn't have anything that was reported stolen in the previous burglaries."

"Maybe the thieves live around here. Maybe they're taking everything to their own place."

"It's possible," Deputy Flick said, "but you'd think a neighbor would notice and get suspicious. Hilltop isn't a big city; people in rural areas tend to know who their neighbors are and what vehicle they drive."

"We've had good media coverage. How could a person carry in load after load without someone wondering about it and putting two and two together?"

"Maybe he unloads at night."

The cell phone rang. Sheriff Alvored answered.

"This is Alex Kendrill. I found a bag of trash in our garbage can that isn't ours. There were two pieces of paper in it; one has our phone number on it and the other has an address."

"What's the address?"

"Six thirty-five West Platt."

The sheriff repeated the address while his deputy wrote it down.

"Thanks, Alex," Sheriff Alvored said. "We'll check it out."

Deputy Flick called headquarters and asked who lived at that address.

Sheriff Alvored pulled away from the curb. "We aren't too far from West Platt now," he said.

Soon Deputy Harper's voice came over the radio: "I have the information you wanted on that address. It's a big storage complex called Overflow Storage."

"It makes sense," the sheriff said as he drove. "The thieves take all the stolen goods to one of those rental units, and leave it for a couple of months until the owners have quit watching the want ads or searching the pawnshops for their stolen items. Then the thieves take the items out of storage and sell them."

"Sounds reasonable."

"It always bothers me when there's a child involved," Sheriff Alvored said. "Makes me think of my own kids."

"Me, too. I wonder why they took the boy, if they did, and what they'll do with him."

Sheriff Alvored did not reply. He didn't want to say what he thought would happen.

He didn't need to.

"We have to find that boy," Deputy Flick said, "before it's too late."

18

Benjie kept counting. He was up to three hundred eighteen when he heard tires approaching on the gravel. Was it the van returning, or was it a different car. Someone who could help him? He wished he could see outside the dryer.

He heard the tires stop next to his hiding place.

Maybe it wasn't the bad guys. Maybe it was the people who owned the washer and dryer. Hope leaped high in Benjie's chest, but he didn't push the door open. Not yet. He had to be sure who was out there.

"What did I tell you? Sitting there waiting for us."

Benjie's hope turned to despair as he recognized Vance's voice.

He could tell that the men had left the van's engine running. Their footsteps crunched on the gravel as they walked toward the dryer.

Did they know he was inside?

Why else would they be coming?

He barely breathed as he listened to the men approach.

The footsteps stopped.

"Take the washer first," Vance said. "Lift on the count of three."

They don't know I'm in here, Benjie thought. If they knew, they would open the door and make me get out.

"One, two, three!"

Benjie heard a scraping sound against the outside of the dryer. He heard one of the men grunt, the way men do when they're lifting something heavy.

"It's leaking," Porker said. "Water came out of the hose and got my shoe all wet."

"Lift a little higher," Vance said. "Slide it in."

Benjie realized the men were putting the clothes washer in their van. They hadn't come back for Benjie; they were stealing the appliances.

He wished he had pulled the dryer door all the way shut. What if it swung open when they picked up the dryer? What if one of the men looked inside and saw him?

He didn't dare close the door now. They might see it move or hear the click as it closed. He would have to sit here like an animal in a cage, and wait.

"Now the dryer," Vance said.

What would happen if the men found him? Scary images rattled in Benjie's brain like coins in a piggy bank.

A boot kicked the dryer door from the outside. Startled, Benjie's hands flew to his mouth, stifling a gasp. The door clicked shut.

"Lift when I count three," Vance said. "One, two, three." Benjie felt himself rise, as if he were in an elevator.

"This dryer is heavy," Porker complained. "Are you sure it's empty?"

Don't look, Benjie thought. Please, please, don't open the door and look inside.

"Quit your bellyaching," Vance said, "and move it."

"We should have brought the truck. It's easier to load."

Benjie pushed his hands against the dryer drum in front of him and braced his back on the inner ridges, trying not to bump against the door as the men tilted the dryer and lifted it into their van.

He heard the van doors close and felt the van move forward. In only a minute or two the van stopped, the door opened, and Benjie heard the door on the storage unit roll up. Even without being able to see, Benjie knew exactly where he was, and what was going to happen next.

They took the dryer out first.

Once again Benjie managed not to bump against the door or make any sound while the two men lifted the dryer from the van and carried it inside the storage unit.

Instead of setting the dryer down gently, Porker let go of his side when it was a foot from the cement floor.

Crash!

A sharp pain jolted up the back of Benjie's neck when the dryer landed. His head snapped back and hit the metal drum.

"Ooof!" The sound escaped even though he was trying to be quiet.

"What was that?" Porker said.

Tears stung Benjie's eyes as he waited for the door to be flung open.

"That was the dryer getting dented, you oaf," Vance said. "You're supposed to put it down carefully, not drop it."

"I couldn't hold it any longer. I told you I was too tired to do this."

"For someone who calls himself a muscle man, you sure are a wimp."

Muscle man? Benjie frowned. The men who had moved the furniture for Mary and Mrs. Sunburg were called Muscle Men Movers. Is that who the burglars were?

A minute later Benjie heard another sharp clunk on the concrete and knew the washer had been unloaded, too.

"Let's get out of here," Vance said.

"Finally," Porker said.

The overhead door rolled down, and Benjie heard the van drive away.

The men were gone.

Benjie went limp with relief. He remained hunched

over in the dryer for a few minutes, to be sure they didn't come back. He thought about how close he had come to being discovered.

He also thought about the possibility that these two men ran a moving company as a way to see what people owned. Then, after they got paid as movers, they went back and stole the expensive things. They would know exactly what was there.

Of course that didn't explain all the burglaries. His family had not hired Muscle Men Movers, and it was three months since Rocky's family had moved. Still, this was important information for the sheriff.

Benjie put his shoulder against the dryer door and pushed, in case the door would release from the inside. The door popped open.

Benjie climbed out. His legs felt wobbly, his neck and shoulders ached, and his hands shook. It was dark inside the storage unit, but Benjie knew the men would have unloaded the washer and dryer right inside the door. He felt in front of him, his hands groping until they hit the metal roll-up door.

He was sure the men would not come back here tonight. It would be safe now for Benjie to leave the storage unit, walk to the street, and find help. He leaned down, his hands feeling along the bottom of the door, searching for a handle.

He dropped to his knees and crawled the full width of the door, feeling along every inch of the door from the bottom to the first hinge, about three feet up. There was no handle, nothing to grasp to roll the door up.

The door only opened from the outside. He was locked in, and nobody knew where he was.

For an instant, panic rose in Benjie. Still kneeling, he beat his fists against the metal door and yelled, "Help! Help!" even though he knew there was no one who could hear him.

Then he took a deep breath and tried to think what a brave and well-trained spy would do in this situation.

Stay calm, he told himself. Listen for a vehicle outside or for people talking, and then yell and pound on the door. He sat on the cold concrete floor and rested his back against the dryer.

He didn't know where he was or how long it would be before someone found him, but he was alive. It was far better to be locked alone in a storage unit than to be on his way to a mountain cabin with two thugs who intended to leave him there to freeze to death.

Benjie's stomach grumbled. He wondered what Mom was fixing for dinner tonight. Spaghetti, maybe? Or tacos? He wondered if Mrs. Sunburg had baked cookies that afternoon. She had asked him what his favorite kind was, and when he had told her snickerdoodles, she had said those were her favorites, too.

His mouth watered at the thought of warm-from-the-oven snickerdoodles. Why hadn't he gone straight to Mrs. Sunburg's house, as he had been told to do, instead of running home when he saw a strange van in his driveway?

Two tears trickled down Benjie's cheeks. He hoped Alex would feed Lizzy for him and clean out her litter pan.

He wondered if Pete had gotten hurt when the bad men threw him out of the van. He hoped not. Pete had tried to help Benjie. He had puffed out his fur and bit the bad man's hand.

Benjie shivered, wishing he had a jacket or a warm blanket. His feet were freezing on the concrete floor, especially the foot with no sock.

He wondered how long it would be before someone went past this storage unit and heard him pounding on the door. Tonight? Tomorrow? Next week?

No. He couldn't think that way. He needed to focus on something positive. Benjie decided to make a mental list of all the information he knew about the burglars. He knew their names, he had written down their license number, he knew what their van looked like. He knew they had used a truck for one burglary and that Porker called himself a muscle man.

Benjie could describe both men. He knew they went hunting and stayed in a cabin in the mountains. He knew a lot about those bad guys. But all of his information wouldn't help him unless he got out of the storage unit.

Benjie remembered that there had been a light on in the storage unit earlier. He stood up and began feeling along the walls, searching for the light switch.

If he could turn the light on, he could look at everything the bad guys had stolen. He could see what was packed in the boxes.

He found the switch and pushed it. The light made him blink. He looked around, feeling less frightened now that it wasn't dark. Maybe there was a cellular phone in here, and he could call for help. Maybe there was an ax, and he could chop a hole in the door. Maybe there was a box of cookies.

19

There's the storage place," Deputy Flick said. "On the right, in the next block. I can see the sign."

Sheriff Alvored slowed the patrol car. "There's a vehicle on the grounds. It's coming out."

"And the driver's in a big hurry," Deputy Flick said.

Sheriff Alvored stopped the patrol car, turned off the lights, and waited.

A maroon-colored van barreled out of the gravel driveway of Overflow Storage, turned right, and sped away.

Sheriff Alvored turned on the lights, stepped on the gas, and followed the van. As soon as the patrol car's lights reached the back of the van, Deputy Flick saw the license number.

"Bingo," he said.

He called their position in to headquarters and requested backup officers as Sheriff Alvored turned on the siren and the flashing lights.

Vance saw the blue lights in the rearview mirror. "We've got cops behind us," he said. "We're being pulled over."

Porker groaned.

"They can't pin anything on us. This is my van and there's nothing in here to connect us to any burglaries. Act innocent. Say we were looking over the storage units because your grandmother died and left you her furniture and you need a place to keep it for a while."

"My grandmother didn't leave me any furniture. My grandmother's healthy as a horse. She's in Reno with her sister."

"Don't say anything," Vance said. "Let me do the talking."

Vance stopped the van and rolled his window down.

Sheriff Alvored approached cautiously. "I'd like to see your driver's license, please," he said.

"Sure thing, Officer." Vance felt in his back pocket, then made a show of feeling his other pockets. "My wallet's gone," he said. "I must have left it in that phone booth."

Deputy Flick and Sheriff Alvored glanced at each other.

"Name?" Sheriff Alvored said.

"Vance Rogers."

Sheriff Alvored looked past the driver, at the passenger. "Do you have any ID?" he asked.

"No," Porker said.

"Your name?"

"Porker Canyon."

"Porker's your legal name?"

"No. That's Beau, but everyone calls me Porker."

"Who've you been fighting with, Porker?"

"I haven't been fighting."

"Your shirt looks as if you've had a tiger on your back, and your hand's bleeding."

"He was wrestling with his nephews," Vance said. "They got a little carried away."

"Do you have the registration for this vehicle?"

"It's in the glove compartment," Vance said.

Porker opened the glove compartment. Something white fell out and dropped to the floor by Porker's feet.

"What was that?" Vance said.

Porker reached down and picked up a child's sock, white with two red stripes around the top. He held it by the toe, letting the other end dangle. "Look at this, Vance," he said.

The deputy pointed his flashlight in the window, illuminating the sock.

"Where's the little boy?" Sheriff Alvored said.

Vance gawked at the sock, looking as surprised as if it had suddenly come to life and begun to sing. "How did that get in there?" he asked.

Porker said, "The kid must have—"

"Shut up, Porker."

"What kid?" said the sheriff.

The two men shrugged.

"I want you both out of the van," Sheriff Alvored said, "with your hands on the roof. Now."

Two more patrol cars pulled up; more deputies surrounded the van as the men did what the sheriff had directed.

Deputy Flick read Vance and Porker their rights while Sheriff Alvored shined his flashlight around the inside of the van. He saw paw prints in the dust on the dashboard. There were a few bits of food wrapper on the floor, along with a tuft of white fur. It looked like cat fur.

Both men denied knowing anything about any burglaries. They claimed they had never seen a small boy and had no idea why a child's sock was in their glove compartment.

"Whose cat has been in your van?" Sheriff Alvored asked.

"We haven't seen any cat," Porker said. "I don't like cats."

"You didn't have a cat in your van?" the sheriff asked.

"What makes you think we had a cat?" Vance asked.

"The paw prints. The white fur."

"Must have been a stray," Vance said. "Probably jumped in through an open window."

"Which one of the storage units do you rent?" Sheriff Alvored asked.

"We want a lawyer," Vance said. "We aren't answering any more questions until we get a lawyer."

"You're going to need one," the sheriff said. He turned

to two of the officers who had just arrived. "Take them in and book them," he said.

"For what?" Vance said. "We haven't done anything."

"Right," Sheriff Alvored said. "You want to explain whose sock that is?"

"You can't arrest us for having a dirty sock in the glove compartment."

"I can when the sock belongs to a missing child," Sheriff Alvored said.

Ten minutes later, with the two men in a squad car on their way to the county jail, Sheriff Alvored and Deputy Flick turned into Overflow Storage and drove slowly past the first row of storage units.

They had already placed a call to the manager, who was on her way in case they needed to open one of the units. The manager said she had a list of all the people who rented storage units and would print it out as soon as she got there. She didn't remember anyone named Porker Canyen, but Vance Rogers sounded familiar; she thought he was two months behind in paying rent, but she didn't remember which unit he had.

"This may be a goose chase," Sheriff Alvored told Deputy Flick. "Even if they put the stolen goods in a storage unit, they wouldn't leave the boy there."

"Not if he was alive."

The patrol car came to the end of the row of storage units, turned, and started down the next row.

"Those two were lying through their teeth," the sheriff said. "They not only had the boy in the van, my guess is that they tangled with the boy's cat. Those scratches and bite marks weren't made by any nephews."

"Let's get out and walk," Deputy Flick said. "If Benjie had enough sense to plant that sock in the glove compartment, he might have dropped some other clue as well, and it's hard to spot anything small unless we're on foot."

The two men got out of the squad car and walked, swinging flashlights in wide arcs.

"Look at this," Sheriff Alvored said. He knelt and examined the gravel.

Deputy Flick looked, too. "Blood?" he asked.

"Looks like it. It's fresh, but there isn't much—a drop every couple of feet."

"Porker Canyen's shoulder was a mess, but I don't think he was bleeding enough to leave a trail," Deputy Flick said.

"This looks more like someone was walking on a cut foot."

The two men looked at each other.

"Someone who wasn't wearing shoes," the sheriff said.

"No shoes and only one of his socks."

They followed the bloodstains to a corner, where they turned and went down a different row of storage units. Twice the red smudges went up close to one of the units, as if the boy had tried to open the door.

They followed the trail around another corner and then, as suddenly as the bloodstains had begun, they stopped.

Both men shined their lights all around that area, but the line of drops had simply ended.

"The ground is wet here," Sheriff Alvored said. He sniffed the gravel. "No odor."

"Maybe we should call in the K-9 team."

They made a note of which unit they were in front of, then continued their search.

When they turned down the next row, Deputy Flick pointed. "Look. I see a sliver of light under that door!"

Both men ran toward the light. As they approached, they called, "Hello! Is anyone in there?"

Fists pounded on the inside of the door. "Help," a voice called. "Help! I'm locked in!"

"Benjie?" Sheriff Alvored called. "Benjie, is that you? This is Sheriff Alvored."

"I'm in here!" Benjie said.

"Are you all right? Someone's coming with a key, but we can break the lock if you need help."

"I'm okay, except I'm cold, and hungry, and my feet hurt."

"I'll go get the squad car," Deputy Flick said. He ran toward where they had left the car.

"We'll have you out of there in a few minutes," Sheriff Alvored said.

Deputy Flick returned with the car.

The manager of Overflow Storage drove up, too.

"We need to get in this unit," Sheriff Alvored said.

The woman used a master key to unlock the door.

When Sheriff Alvored and Deputy Flick rolled up the door, they saw a boy who matched their photo, wearing the clothes his mother had described. He also wore one white sock with red stripes around the top. His face was tear-streaked and his clothes were dirty, but he was unharmed.

"Hello, Benjie," the sheriff said.

"I'm a spy," the boy said, "and I have a lot of important information for you."

Deputy Flick dialed the Kendrills' number.

20

Sheriff Alvored called the Kendrills again after checking the contents of the storage unit. "We not only have your boy," he said, "we have everything the thieves took from your house and from your neighbors. We'll have Benjie home in half an hour. He's requesting a peanut-butter sandwich.

Alex called Mary to tell her the good news, and to invite her and Mrs. Sunburg to come to welcome Benjie home and hear what the sheriff had to say. Rocky called his parents, too.

Now everyone sat in the Kendrills' family room, sipping hot cider and eating the snickerdoodles that Mrs. Sunburg had brought with her.

"Deputy Harper called while we were bringing Benjie home," Sheriff Alvored said. "After Benjie told us about the burglars calling themselves muscle men, we asked her to do some research. She has already found two more unsolved burglaries where the victims or their close neighbors had recently hired Muscle Men Movers."

"That's who moved us!" Mrs. Sunburg said.

"Muscle Men Movers?" Rocky said. "I saw their truck go past on Saturday morning. I remember it because Mom and I laughed about the name."

"What time did you see the truck?" asked Deputy Flick.

"About nine o'clock. My folks and I were going in to town, to go out for breakfast, and the movers drove past just as we left."

"When you got home your house had been burglarized," said Sheriff Alvored.

"Do you think that's who did it?" Rocky asked. "The men with the moving truck?"

"It wasn't a truck at Mary's house the night she was robbed," Alex said. "It was a van."

"They had a van today, too," Benjie said.

"Nine o'clock Saturday is when they were supposed to bring our furniture," Mrs. Sunburg said, "but they didn't show up until noon."

"Maybe they were on their way to Mary's house and they saw Rocky's family leave," Alex said, "so they decided to break in there."

"A crime of opportunity," said Deputy Flick. "They broke in, loaded the stolen goods in their truck, and made a trip to Overflow Storage. Then they came back to deliver the Sunburgs' load."

"I knew those Muscle Men Movers were jerks," Mary said, "when they insulted Pearly."

Pete, who had run under the table when so many people had crowded into the room, came back out and walked toward the sheriff.

Sheriff Alvored eyed him warily.

Pete rubbed his face on the sheriff's shoe. He wound around the sheriff's ankles, purring. This man had found Benjie and brought him home and had put the bad men in jail.

"Is this the same cat that jumped me?" *Sheriff Alvored asked.*

"Yes," Alex said. "This is Pete."

"He seems mellow enough now," *Sheriff Alvored said.* "Earlier, I thought he was a wild cat."

"I'm a mighty jungle beast," *Pete said.*

"Benjie," Mr. Kendrill said, "how did you get so filthy? You look as if you've been mud-wrestling."

Benjie looked down at his shirt and pants. "First I hid in the bushes," he said. "That's where I was when I saw the license number."

"That was good work," the sheriff said.

"I stayed in the bushes until they left," Benjie said. "Then I found out the bad men were stealing Pete. He was in their van, and they were driving away, and I heard Pete crying, and I ran after the van and told them to let him go."

"*I was not crying,*" Pete said. "*I put up a fight. I bit and scratched and tried to rescue Benjie.*"

"I think your cat wants to tell his version of the events," Deputy Flick said.

"I climbed in the truck to get Pete," Benjie continued, "but the men threw him out and made me go with them. Pete was brave; he wanted to stay with me."

"*Benjie was brave, too,*" Pete said. "*He tried to save me, and I tried to save him.*"

"Is Pete hungry?" Mr. Kendrill asked. "Alex, did you remember to feed him?"

"I gave him kitty num-num," Alex said.

"*Could I have some french fries, too?*" Pete asked.

"The suspects deny having a cat in their van," Sheriff Alvored said, "but we saw paw prints and found white fur."

"Pete's missing a hunk of fur," Alex said.

"From the looks of one of the suspects," the sheriff said, "Pete inflicted some damage before they threw him out. The man's T-shirt was shredded across the top, he had deep scratches in his shoulder, and he'd been bit on the hand."

"Way to go, Pete," Alex said.

"*I hope the scratches get infected.*"

"If you have the fur from the van," Benjie said, "we can prove Pete was there." He opened his backpack, removed the envelope marked PETE, and handed it to the sheriff.

"What's this?" Sheriff Alvored asked.

"DNA," Benjie said, "from Pete. You can match it to DNA from the fur in the van."

Looking astonished, the sheriff took the envelope.

"He collected a DNA sample from everyone in our family," Alex explained, "in case bad guys came and kidnapped one of us."

"Benjie, you are a fine spy," Sheriff Alvored said. "That license number in the dirt really helped, and so did the sock in the glove compartment."

"I think we should make Benjie an honorary deputy," Deputy Flick said, and Sheriff Alvored agreed.

Benjie beamed.

Don't forget who found the number in the dirt, Pete said. *"Don't forget who showed it to you."*

"I'm surprised the burglars put their trash in our garbage can," Mrs. Kendrill said.

"They didn't," Mrs. Sunburg said. "I did." She explained.

Lizzy crept into the room. Benjie picked her up and petted her.

"Thanks for making posters about me," Benjie said to Rocky.

"I'm glad we don't need to put up the rest of them," Rocky said. He smiled at Alex.

Making the posters got us through the terrible fear, Alex thought. Instead of crying because we might never see Benjie again, we took action. Mom and Dad went out looking for him; Rocky and I made the posters. We were still afraid, but it helped to do something positive.

"I'm not scared of those bad guys anymore," Benjie said.

"*I never was*," said Pete.

"We can't control what bad people do," Mr. Kendrill said, "but we can choose how we react. You were brave, Benjie. You didn't panic; you used your head."

"So did Alex and Rocky," the sheriff said. "If they hadn't called as soon as they found that address, we might not have caught the men. Another five minutes and they might have ditched the van and gotten away."

"Now that I'm an official deputy," Benjie said, "I'll let you know when I see any flying green panthers."

"You do that," said Sheriff Alvored.

"Maybe I'll even see a flying green possum, and it can be Pearly's friend."

"Pearly's going to be released tomorrow," Mary said. "Gramma's driving her to the wildlife center, and they'll take her into the woods."

"I'm glad you didn't try to keep her," Alex said.

"So am I," Mary said.

"Are you going to keep Rufus?" Rocky asked.

"No," Mrs. Sunburg said. "We do foster care. When Rufus heals, we'll find a good home for him."

Rocky turned to his parents. "Could I adopt Rufus?" he asked. "He has only three legs, but he's a great dog."

Rocky's mom and stepdad looked at each other, then spoke at the same time. "Yes," they said.

Pete looked around the room. Everyone was relaxed and smiling. Even the sheriff and the deputy lounged comfortably on the couch. Pete's tail swished. It was the perfect time for a cat fit.

He leaped into the air and came down beside the sheriff. He skimmed the top of the deputy's shoes, dashed out of the room, made a U-turn in the hallway, raced back to the family room, and catapulted toward the media center.

He landed on the empty shelf where the television belonged. "Did you see that?" he hollered. "I'm a catapulting cat!"

"Gracious," Mrs. Sunburg said.

"He shot up there as if he came out of a catapult," Sheriff Alvored said.

"Yes!" Pete shouted. "Say that again!"

"We were right the first time," Deputy Flick said.

"He's wild," agreed the sheriff.

Lizzy looked at Pete, leaped off Benjie's lap, and climbed the drapes.